The birdgirl was seated before them,
still singing as she combed her hair.

"Handbright," said Mavin, in a husky whisper.
"Handbright. It's Mavin."

The birdgirl slowly turned her head so she could
see them where they stood. She was dressed in a
soft green robe, the color of the noonglow, with
ribbons of blue and silver in her hair. Her face was
bony, narrow, like the face of a bird. She looked
like something out of the old tales, thought
Beedie, something remote and marvelously beautiful, too wonderful to be human. And yet, this
Mavin spoke to her. . . .

"Handbright. Sister. See, it's me, Mavin. Come
all the way from the lands of the True Game, from
Schlaizy Noithn, over the boundless sea to find
you."

Ace Fantasy Books by Sheri S. Tepper

THE REVENANTS

The Books of the True Game
KING'S BLOOD FOUR
NECROMANCER NINE
WIZARD'S ELEVEN
THE SONG OF MAVIN MANYSHAPED
THE FLIGHT OF MAVIN MANYSHAPED
THE SEARCH OF MAVIN MANYSHAPED
(coming in September '85)

THE FLIGHT OF
MAVIN MANYSHAPED

SHERI S. TEPPER

ACE FANTASY BOOKS
NEW YORK

THE FLIGHT OF MAVIN MANYSHAPED

An Ace Fantasy Book / published by arrangement with
the author

PRINTING HISTORY
Ace Original / June 1985

ISBN: 0-441-24092-5

Ace Fantasy Books are published by The Berkley Publishing Group,
200 Madison Avenue, New York, New York 10016.
PRINTED IN THE UNITED STATES OF AMERICA

Chapter 1

From her perch on the side of the mainroot, Beedie could lean back at minor peril to her life and look up the Wall, the mainroot dwindling away in perspective until the solid, armspan width of it had shrunk down to a mere hair's breadth line at the rim of the chasm. So much height above was dizzying, and she slapped at the right piton to hear the comforting thwunging sound which indicated it was solidly set. Setting her spurs more deeply into the bark, she thrust back against the strap to look up once more at the light falling through the leaves of the flattrees, huge even at this distance, a ten-day climb from the rim. She didn't want to miss the noonglow, that vivid, emerald moment when the light came directly down through the leaves, making the whole chasm shine with the same verdant light it now shed on the western, morning-light, wall. Sometimes birds could be seen in the noonglow, enormous white ones, messengers—so the Birders said—of the Boundless.

It was in the noonglow that the birdwoman had come,

slanting down in the green rays, white plumes streaming
from the edges of her wings, to alight on the bridge rail
of Topbridge, almost within the arms of Mercald the
Birder. And Mercald had had her ever since, ever since
he caged her that day only to find a girl in the cage the
following morning. It had been either bird or girl every
day since, with no one able to say for sure what it meant
or why she had come in the first place. Still, the Birder
caste had gained more status from that event than they
had in all the history of the bridges—so much so that
there was serious consideration of elevating them to the
same high status as the Bridgers, Beedie's own caste.
Not that she cared.

"Not that I care," she advised herself. "It makes no
difference to me," knowing that it made considerable
difference to some. There were three Bridger families in
the chasm, and while the Beeds and the Chafers were
not jealous of caste status, the Banders certainly were.
She would bet that old Slysaw Bander would do
everything in his power to prevent any Birder being considered *his* equal. "Thank the Boundless he isn't the
eldest," she reflected. "If old Slysaw were the eldest,
the whole chasm would regret it."

Judging noonglow to be some time off yet, she dug in
her spurs and began climbing upward; chuff, heave,
chuff, heave, chuff. The roll of measuring cord at her
belt had unreeled almost to its end. Chuff, heave, chuff.
Left, right, heave the strap, left, right, heave the strap.
The measuring cord began to tug. She leaned out on her
strap once more, judging how close she had come to her
starting mark. Immodest self-congratulations. Within
an arm's reach; not bad. She began to set pitons on the
mark, right and left. Might as well set them deep. She
would be back to this place with others of the Bridgers
soon, getting ready to set the lines, tackle and winches.
Topbridge had become crowded, too crowded, many
thought, and the elders wanted the bridgetown widened.
Even from this distance she could hear the sounds of
the crowd from Topbridge, cries from the market, the
rasp of a saw from the middle of the bridge where the

Crafters House stood, hammers banging on anvils. She took up her own hammer, concentrating on the job. When the pitons were set deeply she leaned on her strap once more, waiting for the noonglow.

High above the bridgetowns the rim of the chasm was edged with flattrees, wider than they were high, one set of roots anchoring the trees to the rock of the plain, another set dropping down the chasm wall into the dark pit of the bottom with its unseen mysterious waters. Here and there the mainroots bulged into swollen, spherical water-bellies, sole source of water for the bridge people. At intervals the mainroots sent out side roots, smaller though still huge, which grew horizontally along the wall before plummeting downward. The side roots put out ropey, smaller roots of their own, and the ropey roots were heavily furred in hair roots, the whole gigantic mass curtaining the sides of the chasm like a monstrous combed pelt, a matted shag of roots so dense that none of the chasm wall could be seen. In shadow, the roots appeared dark and impenetrable, but now in the emerald light of glorious noonglow the shaggy mass blazed out of shadow in jeweled greens as bright as the high glowing leaves, each strand an individual shining line. A chorus of floppers began to honk somewhere in the mass; flocks of birds broke from the distant rim to circle in the light like devotees circling the altar of the Boundless. All the noises of Topbridge ceased—the other cities were too far down to be heard except as a murmur—the sound of the bell and the call to prayer coming from the Birder's tower in a thin, cutting cry, sharp as broken glass.

Below her right foot she could see the Bridger house of Topbridge and the bridge itself, wide and solid, diminishing into a long wedge stretching across the chasm to the far wall, 2000 paces away. On either side of it were nets looking like lace, dotted with the fallen flattree leaves they were put there to catch.

Below her left foot she could see the narrower wedge of Nextdown, too tiny to seem real, and beyond it to the left, up-chasm, the thin line of Midwall. Down there somewhere lay Bottommost, barely visible, shining sometimes at noonglow as the merest thread. Potter's bridge and Miner's bridge were up-chasm, hidden by the bulk of Topbridge, but she could see Harvester's far off to her right, just at the place the chasm began to turn away west. Seven cities of the chasm. And the broken one above. And the lost one below. The lost one which had disappeared, so it was said, all in one night into the depths of the chasm together with all its people and all its fabled treasure—punished, the Birders said, because of some insult to the Boundless. Lately, though, there had been talk of other reasons, perhaps other bridgetowns in jeopardy—talk of something down in the depths which threatened them all. She made a religious gesture, a ritual shiver at the thought of the lost bridge, then put it out of mind.

The Birder had finished calling prayers. Already the glow had moved from morning wall to evening wall. Time to get on with the task.

She had begun the job the day before by climbing the great mainroot which supported Topbridge in order to measure it from midpoint to the place it left the wall in its long catenary. She had started early in the morning, shivering a little in the mists at the edge of Topbridge commons as she fastened on her belt and spurs. None of the Bridgers had been out and about yet. She had touched the bell outside the Maintainer's door as she came by, and a 'Tainer had come running—or giving that appearance. Hairroot Chafer gave as his opinion that 'Tainers were bred for slowness, like the slow-girules the Harvesters used to gather root nodules, and only gave the impression of running by leaning forward, wherever they went—to give her a cup of nodule broth and a crisp cake of wall moss.

"A fine morning, Bridger." It was the Maintainer called Roges, a tall, strong man, who seemed often to be the one available when Beedie needed something.

"Fine enough," she had answered shortly. It did not do, she had been told, to become too friendly with the Maintainers. Pity. This one seemed to have good sense and he was not slow, no matter what Hairroot Chafer said. "I seem to be about the business early."

"It was the Birder feast last night," the Maintainer murmured, looking politely away while she finished the broth. "To discuss the elevation of the Birder caste. Everyone drank a great deal. You had not yet returned from the mainroot, Bridger." Though he did not breach courtesy, she could tell he was curious about that. She toyed with the idea of making up some story to keep the 'Tainers occupied in myth-building for a day or two—everyone knew they were frightfully superstitious—but her sense of fairness prevented.

"I broke a spur, 'Tainer. Unfortunately, I also broke the strap. I had a spare spur, as what Bridger would not, but not a spare strap, and it took a little time to braid one out of root hair." She was a little embarrassed at his look of concern. A broken strap was nothing. "True, I was late returning. Was it you put the meat and moss cake by my bed?"

He nodded. "I saw you had not returned. It is difficult to sleep if one is hungry."

"And difficult to sleep if a hungry Bridger comes hammering on your door," she said, grinning. Roges must have been thinking of his own sleep as much as of hers. She handed him the cup, checked the fastening on her belt, then began to climb the side root. The great mainroot of the city was only a little above her head at this point.

"May the roots support you as they do the city," the 'Tainer called from below, looking up after her for longer than necessary before moving away toward his house. Beedie did not reply. Getting from the side root to the mainroot took a bit of tricky maneuver, and she wanted her attention on her work. Once on the top of the mainroot, she fastened the end of her measuring cord to the root just over the bulge that marked the center point and then began to walk along the root toward the evening light wall, slightly uphill. When the curve grew steeper she threw her strap around the root, dug in her spurs and started to climb, the measuring cord unreeling from its container at her waist. It was a good climb, steeper the closer to the wall she came, higher and higher above the bridgetown, until at last she could reach out and touch the wall through the tangle of rope roots and hairs. She marked the place.

Now she had to locate a new mainroot, one straight and supple, with no soft spots or water-bellies, and measure it downward from a place on the wall even with her mark, her own white-painted signs which showed bright even against the shadow. She had spent the rest of the day prospecting among the likely mainroots for the best possible one as close to the existing bridge as possible. That had been yesterday's work.

Today she had started early again, climbing to the mainroot she had selected and marking it carefully. She fastened her measuring cord at that point, then climbed down as she checked each arm-length of the root for imperfections. Sometimes a mainroot would look solid, with unblemished bark, but there would be soft spots hidden away. One tapped with the hammer while listening for the telltale dullness, the soggy sound which would hint at rot. One tapped and listened, tapped and listened, and then one prayed anyhow, for there were rots set so deep no Bridger could find them except by luck and the help of the Boundless. The root she had chosen seemed good throughout its length. She had fastened her cord at the bottom and climbed back up the root, measuring once more to come to her present perch. "Measure twice, cut once," she told herself wearily. Bridger youngsters were reared on the story of Amblebee Bridger who measured once, cut once, and found he had cut too short the only mainroot near enough to use. "Measure twice, cut once." Well, she had measured twice, and tomorrow she would start preparing for the cut. She thwapped the pitons with her hand one final time, then started the climb down. On the far side of the chasm, Byle Bander should have completed his own measurement today. Likely he would be preparing to cut soon as well.

After they were cut, the two great roots would be hauled up, the cut ends rising, coming closer and closer in the middle of the chasm until they almost touched. Then one end would be shaped into a socket, the other into a join, the join would be doused with plant glue, the two would be hauled together and secured with lines while they grew together. In a couple of seasons the join would be callused over, bulging a little, stronger than the mainroot itself.

She hoped Byle Bander would cut his mainroot long enough to make a good socket. Last time he hadn't left enough to allow chopping away all the wood they had set hooks into, and roots made a better join if all the hook-damaged wood was cut away before socketing. Last time had only been a side root, one meant to carry a footbridge and stairs between Topbridge and Nextdown. It hadn't had to carry much weight. Still—it would have been better to cut a little longer. And a mainroot, one meant to carry a city, well—she just hoped he cut it long enough. It wouldn't do to suggest it to him. Though Byle Bander had received his tools and titles in the same season Beedie had, to hear him talk he'd been rootwalking two lifetimes at least. Any thought of Byle Bander made her uncomfortable and brought back a memory of the summer that the root broke, one she would rather not have recalled.

The summer the root broke, Beedie had been about ten, living in the Bridger House on Nextdown with her father, Hookset, her mother, Rootwalker, and assorted aunts, uncles, cousins and remoter kin. Uncle Highspurs was the eldest Bridger on Nextdown, which made the Beed family head of caste and main occupiers of Bridgers House. The other Bridger family on Nextdown was the Bander family who said they preferred to live by themselves in a wallhouse at the far, evening-light, side of the chasm. They had moved up from Midwall, some said, though others thought it was from Bottommost itself, and they did not talk as the Nextdowners did. There were only half a dozen Banders in the family: Slysaw and his wife, two grown sons, one old aunt and a boy Beedie's age, Byle. There were known to be many more members of the Bander family at Topbridge, and still more at Miner's bridge, but the family at Nextdown was neither numerous nor considered very important. Beedie thought about that sometimes, how common and unimportant the Banders had seemed.

The elders had decided to expand Nextdown on the up-chasm side. The discussions about it had gone on for a long time, at least a season, with a good deal of exploration among the mainroots to locate proper candidates to carry the new part of the bridgetown. Beedie had even been allowed to try her own little spurs up and down the roots, being shown the water-bellies and how to find soft spots, learning how to judge the direction of side roots. Both the first and second pair of support roots had been located, and the first pair was due to be cut, morning-light side first, then the evening-light side. The Beed family had made the decisions, but they'd invited old Bander, him they called Slysaw, to be part of the cutting crew. He'd told them no thank you very much, but his family had planned to visit kin downstairs at Potters' bridge that day and some days to follow.

"Besides, you Beeders have plenty hands," the man had said, sneering a little, the way he always did. "Mighty prolific family, the Beeders. You've got hands aplenty. Just take Highspurs and Hookset and a few uncles and you've got the job done in a jiffy." Then he and his family had gone off to the stairs, seeming eager to make the two-day climb it would take with the old woman, though the younger ones might have made it in a day, going down.

"Well," said Beedie's dad. "We offered, 'Walker. You heard me make the offer. The old fart won't cooperate worth a flopper's honk. We try and make work for him to earn his space and he goes to visit kin. We don't make work for him and he complains to the elders we're shutting him out. Don't know what would satisfy the Bander family, tell true, and I'm about tired of trying to find out."

Beedie remembered it, all of it, the conversation

around the hearth where the deadroot fire gleamed and the 'Tainers were stirring the soup pot. Next morning six of the Beeds, including Uncle Highspurs and Beedie's parents, went down-root to make the cut, and that was the last anyone saw of them, ever. Hookset and Rootwalker. Uncle Cleancut, Uncle Highspurs, Cousin Rootcutter, Cousin Highclimb, the one who had gone all the way to the rim and brought back most of a fresh leaf from a flattree to astonish them all with the color of it when she unfolded it and it covered the bridgetown from side to side.

All the elders of the family were gone, including the eldest Bridger. They had started the cut right enough, but seemingly the root had broken, broken away while they were working, and carried them all to the bottom, into the dark and mystery of the Bounded, among the rejected dead but without the ceremony of the flopperskin kites, the memorial clothes. Six of them, gone, gone with all the tools and the hooks and the lines. All but one rootsaw that Aunt Six found wedged in the cut and brought back to Beedie, for it had been her mother's.

"Something wrong there, Beedie," she had mourned. "That root is all black up inside, as though it had been burned. Looky here at what I found. . . ." She had shown the black lumps. "Charcoal. I took that right out of the root at the back, next to the wall, down a little lower than they started the cut. Oh, from the cut side it looks solid, but from the back, it's only a shell. . . ."

"Daddy wouldn't have cut burning wood," Beedie had objected. "Mother wouldn't. It isn't safe."

"Oh, no, child, they wouldn't have done it. Not if they'd known. If it was burning up inside when they got there, there'd be no smoke to smell. Not until the saw cut through to the center, where the fire was, and then the smoke. . . ." She didn't need to say anything more. Greenroot smoke was lethal. Everyone knew that.

A day later, Beedie had put on her spurs and climbed down against all custom and allowances, for she was too young to be allowed on a mainroot by herself. Still she went, chuff and heave until she thought her arms would drop off, to come at last to the end of the mainroot and see for herself. Someone had been there in the meantime. Someone had chopped away all the char with an adze, leaving only clean root, but Beedie went on down a side root and found pieces of the char caught in the root hairs, back near the wall. She looked down, sick and dizzy from a climb considerably above her strength, seeing not far below her the stair to Potter's bridge. It would have been easy to climb onto the stair from the mainroot. Easy to get to the mainroot from the stair, come to that. Easy. She cut the thought off. Why would anyone burn a mainroot? Greenroot made poisonous smoke. Deadroot was always dried for a long time before burning. Besides, Nextdown needed that root. Meddling with it was unthinkable, so she resolutely did not think it.

The Potter's bridge stairs were so close, so easy in comparison to the long climb upward on spurs that she almost decided to get back to Nextdown that way, but something dissuaded her. Afterward, it was hard to remember what the reason had been, but she connected it to the return of the Bander family that night.

Nothing was the same after that. Slysaw was now the eldest Bridger on Nextdown, which meant he held Bridgers House. He wasn't the most even-handed of holders, either, though elders weren't supposed to play favorites, and it wasn't long before the remaining Beed cousins were moving up to Topbridge or down to Potter's or Midwall. Finally, there had been only Beedie and Aunt Six left, and when old Slysaw told Aunt Six she had to move out of her old rooms because he meant to give them to a Bander cousin from Midwall, Aunt Six decided to leave. The two of them moved up to Topbridge next day, carrying what they could on their backs and leaving the rest for the Banders. "Ill wished on them," said Aunt Six. "Every table and chair ill-wished on them, and may those who sit there have the eternal trots."

On Topbridge the Bridgers were more mixed; there

were some Banders, true, but there were more Beeds and more Chafers and plenty of housing for them all. The Bridgers House was held by Greenfire Chafer—who was killed soon after, some said by a rogue flopper—and Beedie and Aunt Six were given rooms in the Bridgers House at the morning-light end of the bridge right away. Then Beedie got on with her schooling. Still, every now and then she would wake in the chasm night to the sound of floppers honking in the root mat, half dreaming about hiding on the rootwall, lumps of charcoal in her hands, looking up at the adze-cut end of the mainroot while hearing from below that phlegmy chuckle as Slysaw Bander came climbing up the stairs.

And now it was a Bander again, Slysaw's son Byle, come to work on Topbridge, cutting the roots too short, putting his hands on Beedie every chance he got, and bragging as though he were a Firstbridger himself. Beedie wondered, not for the first time, if she and Aunt Six moved to Bottommost whether they might escape from Banders once and for all.

The bridgetown grew larger and louder as she climbed down toward it, chunk, chunk, chunk, the spurs biting into the bark. She felt lucky to have found a mainroot right where it was wanted, with good, clean length and no water-bellies. Sometimes, so she had heard, there were no suitable mainroots within a great distance of the existing bridge. Then it was necessary to build elsewhere, or haul a distant root closer with hooks and ropes, a procedure which took half a lifetime and was as deadly as it was dull. Well, it wouldn't be necessary. As one of the youngest Bridgers, prospecting had been assigned to her, and she had found a good root. That one and the one Byle Bander had found would make up the first pair. After the haulers were started, she'd have to start looking for her half of the second pair. From what the elders had said, this could be a four or five pair job. They wanted the expansion built wide, they said. Enough to absorb all the growth Topbridge might make for the next several lifetimes. Of course, to hear Aunt Six tell it, elders were always like that, always planning more than other people could build. Since the elders didn't actually have to do the job, it was always easy to plan large.

She amused herself going over the steps it would take to make the cut on the morrow, how the Bridgers would ring the root with hatchets, then fit the loop saw into the groove, two of them braced against the root as they pulled alternately, cutting through the mainroot until the whole massive weight of it fell away into the chasm with roaring echoes which seemed to go on forever. It would be the first town root Beedie had helped cut, but she well remembered the sound from the time the root fell at Nextdown. What happened to the roots that fell, she wondered? Did they end up propped against the chasm wall? Or fallen over into the bottom river? Did they rot? Or dry? Did floppers build nests in them? No matter, really. They ended up far below Bottommost, and whatever might happen below Bottommost could not be reckoned with at all. Except, she reminded herself, for whatever this new worry was. Though whether that was coming up from below Bottommost was anyone's guess.

After cutting the root, the Bridgers would bore hook holes in the end of it, set the great hardwood hooks in place, then run rope from the hooks back and forth through the tackle and across the chasm to the hooks set deep in the other root end there. After which everyone on Topbridge would spend a part of their days hauling at the windlass. Everyone, that is, but the Bridgers.

The Bridgers would be making a detailed chart of every side root on the mainroots, every bud, every ropey growth. Once the mainroot was hauled into its long supporting curve, the Bridgers would use many of the verticals hanging from it to support the base of the new bridge. There would have to be other verticals reaching all the way to the distant Bottom and its nourishing waters if the mainroot was to be kept alive and healthy. Still other side roots would be needed for the stairs which were planned to link Topbridge directly to Potter's bridge, replacing the current link by way of Nextdown. Any side roots that didn't fit the plan would have to be trimmed away as they budded; otherwise the mainroot would turn into an unmanageable tangle which could never be maintained properly.

"Hey, skinny girl," came a call from below. She looked down to see Byle Bander leaning from the bridge rail, staring up at her with the half sneer he always wore. "Hey, Beedie, slow-girule. What are you doing, girl? Harvesting nodules?"

There were several slow-girules in the roots nearby, their hooked hands tight around the side roots, moving now and then to clip root nodules from the root with the sharp edges of their claws, like scissors. One just below her had a pouch almost full, and she whispered to it, "Nice giruley. Give us? Give us, hmmm?"

"Hnnn," it growled at her, half in complaint. "Hnnno. Minnnne."

"Ah, come on, giruley. Give us one little root mouse to tide us until supper time. One little juicy one. Hmmm?" She reached out to scratch the creature in the one place its own claws could not reach, the middle of its back. The whine turned into a purr, and the creature handed her a green, furry nodule. She leaned against her belt once more to peel it with her Bridger's knife. Anything for delay's sake. She didn't want to descend with Byle there.

"The Harvesters' caste will be fining you, Beedie," Byle Bander called. "You know you're not supposed to fool with the 'rulies."

"I'm not fooling, I'm hungry," she replied, her mouth half full of the juicy, crunchy root nodule. "I could have picked it myself." If she had behaved in accordance with the rules, she would have picked it for herself. It was uncastely for a Bridger to receive food except from a Maintainer's hands, though the rules did permit harvesting from the roots if one was kept past meal time. The rules did not allow Bridgers to invade Harvesters' caste by taking food from the slow-girules, however, and Beedie flushed. Though it was something all the Bridgers did from time to time, it was precisely the kind of thing Byle Bander would make an issue of, or harass her about until she would be heartily sorry for having done it. He liked to couple his attempts at fondling with threats, and neither were welcome. His presence on the walkway below her made her uncomfortable. Still, delaying any longer wouldn't help. She finished the nodule and wiped her hands on her trousers, moving on down the root to the edge of the bridge. Bander reached out a hand to her, which she ignored. He had the habit of pulling one off balance and then laughing, or, worse, grabbing parts of her she didn't want grabbed.

As she stepped onto the bridge, she saw a group of Bridgers striding toward her at the same time she saw the expression of amused superiority on Byle Bander's face. All of the Bridgers in the group were Banders, interesting in itself. What were they up to?

She waited little time for an answer. One of the Bridgers, a ruddy, fussy little man called Wetwedge, bustled up, peered at her as though he had never seen her before, then said, "You getting ready for the cut, girly?"

"That's what I've been doing," she replied, wondering what this was all about. Certainly it was no chance encounter. It had the feeling of a delegation.

"Not today, girly. No. Big business, this. Got to have it checked at least twice, you know. Can't cut until we check it twice."

"I did," she said, amazed at his open-faced stupidity. What did the man think? That she was witless?

"No, no. I mean you got to have it checked by someone else. Gotcher measuring cord?"

Something deep inside Beedie sat up and looked around with sharp eyes and a sharper nose. Something smelled. "My measuring cord is put away safe, yes."

"Well, trot it out, girly, and we'll check it. Old lady Slicksaw here will climb it down for you, down to your mark, just to check."

"That's not the way it's done," she said, somehow keeping her voice from shaking with anger. "If you want Slicksaw Bander to check my measure, go ahead with my blessing. But she'll use her own cord and compare it to mine before witnesses from Bridgers House, and any difference will be checked by an impartial eye. That's the way it's done, Wetwedge Bander-Bridger, and I'm surprised you should suggest anything different."

The man looked quickly from side to side, seeking support from one or another of them, but they shifted feet uncomfortably, not looking at him. He laughed, trying to put a good face on it. "Well then, takes more time that way, but it's according to rule. So, take a day off, then, Beedie."

She saw deceit on his face, an evil intention which she couldn't read but one made clear in those shifty eyes, darting up and down like a flopper's wings. Besides, he wasn't enough elder to her to tell her to take a day off, and him not even from her own family. "My mark is sealed with my knot," she announced loudly. "Slicksaw can't mistake it." Or alter it, she said to herself. One might mistake an accidental scarring for a hatchet mark, but one would not mistake any accidental tangle in the hair roots for an individual Bridger's own knot, complicated as an alphabet, tied and then doused with paint to make it stand out. "It's tied once at each side, top and bottom," she said. Then, as they began to turn away, "Of course, I'm going to Bridgers House to see that they check Byle Bander's measure as well. Otherwise it would be unfair, wouldn't it, and not something the elders would tolerate. Since you're all Banders checking a Beed, I'll ask the Bridgers House to send Chafers or Beed to check Bander. Fair's fair, after all."

She had the satisfaction of seeing Byle Bander's face full of anger as she stalked away. Nor did she miss the hesitation among the other Banders, the glances, the stuttering lips as one or another of them tried to think of something to say. She did not look back, contenting herself with a call. "Good day to you, Bridgers."

As she walked away to Bridgers House, she could hear their whispers behind her. Well, what had they thought? That she would let a clutter of Bander hangers-on presume to double-check her competence without having some Beed fellows check on Byle's ability as well? Did they think if they called her girly, as they would some curvy Maintainer wench, wriggling her hips between the tables at dinner, that she would not hear what it was they were really saying? Not likely.

She went directly to Bridgers House. She wanted to talk to Rootweaver Beed, second eldest, a white-haired woman with young eyes whom Beedie admired for her good sense and friendly demeanor toward the younger Bridgers. The woman was curled up on a windowseat, weaving carded hairroot fibers to make a new climbing belt.

"Checking you, are they?" Though Rootweaver was not young, she was straight and supple as a side root, and Beedie had seen her using spurs not four days before. Rootweaver considered the matter now, frowning a little. At last her face cleared and she said, "With all the troubles from below we have to worry us just now, leave it to the Banders to come up with something fretting. Well, it's never a bad idea to check a measure, 'specially when it's a mainroot in question. We'll take it as though it were friendly meant and send a crew along to check the Bander whelp as well. Have a day off, Beedie. You might help your Aunt Six with the moving. She's found a place she likes better than Bridgers House again." The woman laughed, not least at Beedie's expression of dismay.

Aunt Six had moved house at least two or three times a year since they had come to Topbridge, never able to settle into the same comfort she had known in the Bridgers House on Nextdown. She had moved into and out of Bridgers House on Topbridge seven times—this would make eight. Having Aunt Six behaving as usual made the day somehow merely annoying, an almost customary irritation taking the place of that extraordinary discomfort she had been feeling since she had been hailed by Byle Bander. If Aunt Six was moving house, it must be assumed the world was much as usual.

So she spent the afternoon with a cart, hauling Aunt Six's bedding and pots and bits and pieces from the pleasant rooms in Bridgers House to some equally pleasant ones on the far edge of Topbridge, about mid-chasm, from which the latticed windows looked out toward Harvester's bridge, a lumpy line against the bend of the chasm wall behind it. Beedie wondered what the view was like from Harvester's. Since it was at the turn of the chasm, could the chasm end be seen from there? Was there a chasm end? Odd. She'd never wondered about that until this very minute.

"Beedie! What are you dreaming about, Bridger-girl? You'll only have this one day to help me, so help me! I've got all the rugs yet to bring."

"Aunt Six, do you think this place will suit you? Will you stay here for a while? Now that I've got my tools and titles, I'd like to get some things of my own for this room, but not if you're just going to move us again."

"Girl, you get your own things and make it your place, you can stay whether I go or not. For Boundless' sake, Beedie. You're a grown-up girl." She compressed her lips into a thin and disapproving line and began to bustle, accomplishing little but giving a fine appearance of activity.

Beedie smiled to herself. The only time Aunt Six referred to Beedie as a grown-up girl was when there was moving to be done, or something else equally boring or heavy. Still, the new place did have that marvelous view of the chasm, being right at the edge this way. Shaking her head, she went to fetch the rugs.

Slicksaw Bander said she found no fault with Beedie's measure. Rootweaver Beed was not so favorable about Byle's. The Beeds found him marked short, as Beedie had feared, and told him so in front of half the Bridgers and a full dozen Maintainers with their ears flapping. Byle was so angry he turned white. Beedie tried not to look superior, failing miserably. Perhaps now he would keep himself to himself and pay attention to his own Bridger business rather than hers. It had a consequence she had not foreseen, however, when she was called to Bridgers House for conference.

"Byle's root was marked short, Beedie," said Root-weaver, the half-dozen assembled Bridger elders behind her nodding and frowning. They had summoned her without warning, always a slightly ominous occurrence, but this time there had been nothing discomforting in it for her. "Not merely a little short," Rootweaver went on, "but far short. As though he had not measured at all, and certainly not twice—or got his cord tangled up on the climb, and that's a child's trick. So we're going to go down there with him tomorrow, check his measuring technique and check his axe work, too. Short in one thing, short in all, isn't that the saying? So. You can go ahead and start cutting a groove on the root you've measured, but we've no one to help you cut root. After we get young Byle straightened out, you'll get your crew. Do what you can alone, and we'll send the crew next day."

"Byle's in the classroom right now," said one of the other elders, indignantly. "Fulminating and fussing. We're keeping him here tonight, doing a little review of technique, and he's mad as a hooked flopper. Madder than he should be. You'd think he'd been planning a lovers' meeting or something the way he's carrying on. Demands to be let go home."

"Bridgers House is home for all Bridgers," said Rootweaver calmly. "Let him go get a change of clothing if he pleases, but I want him to stay here tonight. We'll see if we can't talk some sense into him."

All of this made Beedie quite uncomfortable, and she was glad Byle hadn't seen her with the elders. If he thought she had been privy to his embarrassment, he'd never have permitted her a peaceful day. Since she thought he didn't know, she had a peaceful night. Come morning, though, she thought he had probably found out, for she was visited by a Harvester elder with an annoying sniff and his pen ready to record her words.

"It's been reported you've been interfering with the

slow-girules, girl," he pinch-mouthed at her, pulling his
nose back as though she smelled.

"You may call me Bridger," she said, holding her
fury carefully in check. "And I have never interfered
with a slow-girule in my life. I did take a nodule from
one, yesterday, when I was delayed on the root and
missed a meal."

"Report is you interfered with it. Rassled it about.
Maybe bothered it in its work."

"I scratched its furry back, and it purred at me. So
much for your 'interference.' "

"You could have injured it." The man was white
around the mouth, wanting to storm and yell at her, but
afraid to do so seeing her own anger and knowing what
Bridger wrath meant.

"Nonsense," snapped Aunt Six from behind her.
"You can't injure a slow-girule with an axe. Be done,
Harvester. Beedie took a nodule from one of your
beasties and she must pay a fine for it, for it's against
the rules. So impose your fine and be done. It's no large
thing, and you'd best remember it. The good will of
Bridgers is given freely, but it's taken freely, too, when
there's cause."

The Harvester did not reply, merely threw the piece of
paper at them and stalked away. "Parasites," hissed
Aunt Six, just loud enough that he could not fail to
hear. "No skills of their own, so they must live by
preventing others from using common sense. Sorry the
day the Harvesters ever became a caste, Beedie. And
sorry the day any Bridger takes one like that seriously."

The man heard. He turned and made a threatening
gesture, mouthing something they could not hear.

"Still," Beedie said, "I did break the rule, Aunt Six.
It was seeing that Byle Bander waiting for me on the
bridge, like some old crawly-claw, hiding in a root hole.
I didn't want to come down where he was, so I played
with the 'rulie instead. They like it."

"Of course they like it, child. The Harvesters may
think they own the slow-girules, but no one has ever

convinced a slow-girule of that yet. It's that which makes the Harvesters so angry. They'd like nothing better than to have the 'rulies turn clipper-claws on all except the Harvesters. That would suit them right to the bridge floor. And what kind of a Bridger is Byle Bander to report one of his own caste?''

"A miserable one," Beedie replied in a grim voice. "A miserable bit of flopper flub, for all he's a Bridger."

All this caused Beedie some delay, and it was late in the morning before she started down, chuff, heave, chuff, humming to herself, throwing a glance upward now and then to see if there were birds. It would be wonderful, she thought, to fly like that, up to the flat-trees and the plain—not even dangerous for a bird. A bird wouldn't have to fear the gnarlibars, the giant pombis, the ubiquitous d'bor hiding in every pool and stream, the poison bats, the were owls. A bird wouldn't be bothered by the monsters of the plain, the monsters who had almost wiped out the people, would have wiped them out if they hadn't moved down into the chasm to build the bridgetowns where the monsters couldn't get at them. Not the Firstbridge, of course. That hadn't been built far enough down the chasm, and the monstrous forest pombis had climbed down the mainroots to it as they would have climbed a tree. The site of that disaster was the broken city, still hanging high against the light, a network of black in the up-chasm sky. Then there had been the lost bridge, the one that had disappeared one night, never to be seen again—disappeared between dark and dawn without a sound. Built too low, some said, though legend said it had been built only slightly lower than Bottommost. Trouble in the depths, they said. Then and now, they said. Well, all this conjecture wouldn't help get the job done. She spotted her marks, moved beyond them, readied her hatchet to make the groove, then clung to the root with a sudden, giddy disquietude, overcome by a wave of familiar horror. She had felt like this before. There was something. Something wrong? Something not as usual? Uneasily she shifted on the root, moving around it as a flopper moves when hiding from the hunters, listening to silence, tasting the air, smelling . . . smelling.

What was it? An odor so faint she could hardly detect it? But what? She wished for the crew, the other Bridgers, suddenly aware of her solitude.

She began to move lower on the root, sniffing, tapping at the root with her hammer. The sound was wrong, wrong. She moved lower still, still tapping, then abruptly astonished, feeling the heat beneath her palms as a hallucination, an unreality, outrageous and impossible. Roots were cold, her mind said, and therefore . . . therefore . . .

Even as her mind toyed with a dozen irrelevant notions, her body reacted, leaping upward in three quick movements of arms and legs, chuff, heave, chuff, heave, chuff, hands frantically feeling for cool, not sure they had found it, upward once more in that same panic-ridden gallop, until there was no possibility of mistake. She smelled it then for the first time, that harsh scent of poison smoke, barely detectable. She longed in an instant to be one of the slow-girules, able to turn head down on the root, able somehow to see below her feet. And yet she didn't need to look. She could smell it. The mainroot was burning.

Back in the old times, she had heard, this was the way roots were severed. A Bridger would climb in between the root and the wall, hack away a hole in the root, then put burning charcoal in there to burn away and burn away until the thing dropped. Sometimes the fire didn't go out, however. Sometimes it got into the heartwood and kept on going, poisoning the air, no matter how one cut at it and chopped at it. So the Bridgers had stopped burning roots and began cutting them. But someone had burned a mainroot at Nextdown, and someone had set fire to this one Beedie sat upon, the one Beedie should have arrived at with a full crew of Bridgers, earlier than this. If she went back and told about it the fire would have burned the root away by the time they returned, burned it too high, and it was the only useful one in the right place on this side.

So—so what? So cut it off before it went any further. Cut it off right below the mark, working against time, trying to get it cut through before the fire reached the saw cut and the smoke killed her. Her body began it, even while her mind was thinking through the right procedures. She was high on the root in a moment, setting her pitons and hooks for safety lines, one after the other, running the lines through and down to her belt, checking the buckle, checking the lines, setting them high above the mark, so high that no matter if the root fell, she would be left hanging—if a side root didn't lash her head off, or a tangle tear her away from where she hung.

The axe in her hand flew at the bark, making the first cuts, up and down, overhand, underhand, chips flying out into the chasms to flutter away like crippled birds, down and out of sight forever. The pungent smell of the milky root juice made her nose burn, a corrosive stench. She shifted rapidly to the right, cutting around, keeping her lines straight. When the root was ringed, she went back, doing it again, cutting deep so the saw loop wouldn't slip. Then the hatchet went into the belt, the saw loop came out. She had to throw it from behind the root, with free space all around. She held one handle in her right hand, whipped the length of the saw out and left, praying it would wrap around the root, smacking the handle into her left hand.

No. The saw tangled in a mass of root hairs, dangling. She moved down a little, lashed the saw outward again. The loop spun out, around the root, came back into her waiting left hand with a solid thwack. She eased the blade into the groove, dug her spurs deep and began to pull, right, left, tugging against the saw line with its myriad diamond teeth, seeing the puffs of sawdust fly into the air.

The sawline resisted her for a moment, then bit deep, cutting its own groove deeper, dust puffing at either

side. At first she thought the amount of sawdust ridic-
ulously large, then saw that it was mixed with smoke,
smoke rising in little clouds from the cut, making her
eyes stream, her throat burn. It was deadly. Deadly.
Everything in her urged her to get away, to climb outward, away from that hideous smoke, but instead she
moved around the root to find an updraft of clean air
and went on heaving at the saw. It was well used, supple, only recently reglued with jeweled teeth for which
she had paid a pretty price, the supply of gems being so
short. Aunt Six had always said that good tools repaid
their keeper, and she chanted this to herself as she went
on heaving, feeling the root beneath her spurs begin to
grow warm. The fire was eating its way up, toward the
mark.

"Bite teeth, cut deep, saw line chew, job to do, pull,
Bridger, pull. . . ." then six deep breaths and chant
again, over and over. This was not a job for one
Bridger! She should have had a full crew, spelling one
another as they tired, encouraging one another. "Bite
teeth . . ." It was getting a little easier as the groove bit
deeper, there was less surface to pull against. "Bite
teeth, cut deep, saw line chew. . . ." In older days, there
had been plenty of gems, plenty of saw gravel. Maybe
she should have paid for another dipping. Pull. Pull.
The root quivered.

Quickly she shifted her feet upward, bracing out
above the groove, lying almost horizontally from the
root as she heaved the line, heaved, heaved, feeling her
shoulders start to burn and bind, beginning to choke in
the smoke once more, unable to move from this stance,
unable to shift her position, trying to hold her breath
against that one too many which would bring the poison
full strength deep into her lungs.

A quiver again, this time a mighty one, a shaking, a
groaning sound, a rending as the world began to drop
from beneath her. The root below her fell away—but
only a finger's width, whipping the entire root to one
side as it did so, throwing her to the end of her lines,
breaking two of them with lashing side roots. She hung,

nose dripping blood, suspended between her remaining two lines, turning like a hooked flopper, gagging at the smoke. One incredibly strong cable of fiber held the root, kept it from falling away, one bundle no thicker than her leg, groaning as though it had human voice, toward which the fire crept, upward, upward—taking what seemed an eternity to burn it through.

She fainted, came to herself, began to go in and out of blackness as though it were a garment put on and took off. Through a veil of swimming gray she saw the mass of the mainroot dropped away down the endless depth of the chasm, lashing side roots as it went so that they twitched and recoiled, knocking Beedie against their rough sides. She swung still at the end of her lines, thrashed into semiconsciousness, eyes staring upward at the rim.

Far above the noonglow came, through emerald light, a kind of singing. Was it the Birder on Topbridge or the singing of her own blood? High in the light she saw wings, white wings, circling down and down, huge and mysterious, wonderful as a myth, beautiful as a song.

"It will stop at Topbridge," she told herself in her dream, "like the other one." But it did not. It came down and down until it perched on a side root spur just beside her and turned into something else. Something with a woman's face, but with hands and arms like a slow-girule, arms to hold fast, and legs to reach out and pick Beedie from her lines as though she had been no heavier than a baby. Then the bird person wiped the blood from her face and cradled her, cradled her there on the root and whispered to her.

"My name is Mavin, little root climber. It seems to me you need some help here, whatever strange wonderful thing it is you are so determined to do."

Chapter 2

After a time Beedie came to herself lying on a horizontal shelf of side root, carefully fastened to it with her own belt and pitons, having the blood washed from her face and neck with something that looked suspiciously like a furry, wet paw. The paw owner went away. There was a sound of water near by, splashing and trickling, then Beedie's head was lifted and a cup thrust at her lip. She drank, trying not to look at the cup, for it had appeared magically where the paw had been. When the paw/cup/person retreated from her side again, she turned her head to follow the creature/woman/bird as it went to the water-belly and burrowed into it through a sizeable hole in the tough shell which had not been there when Beedie had passed it earlier in the day.

"How did you cut it?" she asked, her voice a mere croak in the sound-deadening mat of the rootwall. "It takes a drill, and a blade saw. . . ."

"Or a sharp beak and determination," said the bird/person/creature. "You reached toward this place when I carried you past, mumbling something or other about

25

being thirsty, so I figured there was water inside this
what you call it. . . ."

"It's a water-belly," Beedie murmured. "It stores
the water the root brings up from the bottom, down
there. . . ."

"Down there, eh? A very long way, root climber. Do
you go down there often?"

"Never." She shook her head and was frozen into im-
mobility by the resultant pain. "Never. No. Too far.
Too dark. The Boundless punished the Lostbridgers by
sending them down there, so they say. Maybe for greed,
because of the gemstones. We're running out, you
know. All the ones left from that time have been used
up. Dangerous. Dangerous creatures on the Bottom,
they say. As dangerous as the plain, up top, where you
came from."

"Plenty of creatures up there, all right. Gnarlibars.
Pombis bigger than any I've seen elsewhere. There's a
kind of giant bunwit with horns on its rear feet, did you
know that? Strangest-looking thing I've ever seen. And
I've seen wonders, oh, root dangler, but I've seen
wonders. Oceans and lands, lakes and forests, all and
everything in a wide world full of wonders. Among
which, may I say, is this place of yours, what you call
it?"

"The chasm? We just call it the chasm, that's all." If
Beedie lay perfectly still, she could speak without really
feeling discomfort. So she assured herself, at least.

"Do you know what it looks like from up there?" the
bird/woman/person asked. "Let me tell you, it's a
remarkable sight. To start with, the roots from those
trees extend out onto the plain like great cables, bare as
pipes. I saw them from up there, my soaring place, and
had to come down just to see my eyes didn't lie to me.
Leagues and leagues of these great roots laid out side by
side, like the warp threads of some giant loom all ready
for the weaving. Then, after leagues of nothing but bare
root, a few little stalks pop up; short, stubby things,
with one leaf, maybe, or two, gossamer leaves, spread
to the sun like the wings of something bigger than you

can imagine. Then the stalks grow higher, higher yet, bigger and bigger, until all you can see is the leaves, overlapping each other like scales on a fish, thin as tissue, and green—Gamelords, girl, but it's a lovely green."

"I know," murmured Beedie, entranced by the rough music of that voice. "We see it every day, at noon-glow."

"And then a shadow in the green, slightly darker, with a mist rising up through it. At first I thought it was only a river under there, but then I saw how wide the shadow was, a long, dark stripe on the forest, going away north to tall, white-iced mountains; bending away to the southwest into a desert hot and hard as brass, and that mist coming up full of food smells and people smells.

"Well, I came down, girl, working my way down through those gossamer leaves, eyes all sharpened to see what I could see far down, and what should I see but this great root thrashing about and a small girl person hung on it being smoked like a sausage, the smoke roiling nasty to my nose."

"I saw you coming down," said Beedie. "At first I thought I was dreaming it, that you were the other one."

There was a long silence, then the bird/creature/person said, in a voice even Beedie recognized as carefully noncommital, "What other one is that?"

"The white bird. The great white bird who came down, oh, a long time ago. A year, almost. It came down in the noonglow, and it perched on the railing of Topbridge commons. Mercald was there, Mercald the Birder?" She started to make an inquiring gesture, to move her head questioningly, but desisted at the swimming nausea she felt. The expression on the bird/person's face had already told her it did not know what Birders were. "White birds are the messengers of the Boundless, you know?" Beedie tried again. The bird/person nodded helpfully, indicating this was not impossible. "And the Birders are the servants of the

Boundless. They do our judging, and our rituals, and
dedicate the festivals, things like that. So, birds being
sacred, and Mercald being a Birder, naturally, he took
the white bird to the Birders House. Only later on it
changed into a person, a woman. Like you did."

"Ah," said the bird/person in a flat, incurious voice.
"Tell me your name, will you girl? And call me by mine.
It will make it easier on us both. I'm Mavin."

"Mavin," said Beedie. "I'm Beedie. Beed's daughter, really, but they call me Beedie. I'll get some other
kind of name after I've worked at Bridging a while—
something like, oh . . ."

"Smoked sausage? Root dangler?"

"Probably." She raised one trembling hand to feel
along her ribs. They were bruised, terribly tender, and it
hurt when she took a deep breath or moved her head.
She put the hand down, carefully, and was still once
more. "More likely something like "Rulie-chaser' or
'Strap-weaver.' We like to be named after big things
we've done, but some of us never do anything that big."

"Well, Beedie, what did this other bird have to say
for itself? When it changed into a woman, I mean?"

"It never said anything, not that I heard of." The
question made her a little uncomfortable, as though
there were a right answer to it, one she didn't know. "It
sings. Mercald used to bring it out in the noonglow and
it flew. It circled around and around in the light,
singing. Lately, though, it hasn't changed into a bird at
all. It's stayed a woman."

"What does the woman do?"

"Sits. She sits in the window of the Birders House
and brushes her hair. They feed her fruit and moss
cakes, and bits of toasted flopper. They give her nodule
beer to drink, and water. They dress her in soft dresses
with ribbons woven by the Weavers' caste, especially for
her. At festival times she watches the processions, and
the jugglers, and the root walkers. And she sings."

"And never speaks? Never at all?"

"Never at all," said Beedie, in a definite voice. "Now,

best you tell me what she is to you, for the people up there"—she moved her eyes to indicate the woven bottom of the great bridge above which threw an enormous shadow across them— "those people think she's sacred. You go asking too many questions, like you have with me, and they won't be contented just wondering where you came from, like I do. They'll wonder if maybe you're a devil from the Bottom. Or another messenger from the Boundless, in which case they'll lock you up, just to keep you safe, until they decide you've delivered the message, whatever it's supposed to be." She fell into a gray fog, exhausted by this speech.

"Dangerous, then, to be a messenger! Well, who else could I be? Who could visit you without stirring any curiosity at all?"

Beedie's head was swimming, but she tried to consider the question carefully. "You could be someone from Harvester's bridge. We hardly ever see anyone from Harvester's, because it's such a long way down-chasm. There's a Harvesters House on Topbridge, so you'd have someplace to stay." She sighed, the pain pulsing insistently.

"Ah. Well now. Tell me, Beedie, do you owe me for saving your life?"

She had not thought about it until that moment, and it was an odd question, all things taken into account, but still it was a question she could answer. "Yes," she said. "I owe you."

"Good. I want you to tell me all about this place, the chasm, the—what did you call them?—the bridge-towns. About Harvesters and Bridgers and whatever else there are about. Then, when you've done that, you won't owe me anymore and· we can talk about some other arrangement."

"You're . . . strange," Beedie commented. "If you hadn't pulled me off that root and got me out of the smoke, I'd be dead by now, though, so I guess strange doesn't matter."

"A remarkable conclusion for one so young. So,

sausage girl, tell me about this place. I am a stranger. I know nothing. You must tell me everything, even the things you know so well you never think of them.''

It was an odd session, one Beedie was always to remember. Later in her life, the memory was evoked by smoke smell, always, or by sudden jolts of pain. Even after, she was to recall this time whenever she was ill or injured. Now she lay as quietly as she could on a furry root, soft as her own bed, cushioned somehow in the arms or person of whoever it was called herself Mavin, and talked through her pain about the chasm, sometimes as though she were present, sometimes as though she were dreaming, in both cases as she had never talked or heard anyone talk before.

"Our people came here generations ago," she said. "Down from the plain above. I didn't know about the trees and the roots up there, because all the records of that time were lost when Firstbridge was destroyed. All we know is that the people were getting eaten up by the beasts, so the Firstbridgers came down into the chasm and built a bridge. Firstbridge. It wasn't far enough down, and the beasts got at it, so the survivors came down further to Nextdown while they built Topbridge. You can see Firstbridge if you look, way up against the light. We call it Brokenbridge sometimes. There isn't much left of it but the mainroots and a few dangling verticals. When my cousin Highclimb went to the rim, she saw it. She says the mainroots are still alive.''

"Ah. Humm. Are there any—ah—Gamesmen, among you?"

"Gamesmen? You mean people who play games? Children do, of course. There are gambling games, too. Is that what you mean?"

"Are there any among you who can change shape? Who can fly? Who can lift things without using their hands?"

"Demons, you mean. No. There's a story that before we came down into the chasm, there were Demons or something like that over the sea. We used to trade with them in the story, but it's only a story. According to the story, we came to this world before they did. When we came, the animals weren't so bad, so we lived on top. Then, later, the animals got bad. That's when we moved down.''

"All of you? All the persons this side of the sea?"

Beedie shook her head and winced. "I don't know. I don't think anyone knows. We keep hearing stories about lost bridges or lost castes. People who survived some other way. Aunt Six says it's all myths, but I don't really know. Do you still want to hear more about the chasm?''

"I didn't mean to interrupt. It was just a thought. Yes, go on.''

"Well, let's see. After Topbridge was built, they finished Nextdown. Then the Potters built their bridge down-chasm, because there were clay deposits in the wall along there, and coal. They use that for the firing. Then came Miner's bridge, further down-chasm, because that's where the mines were. Metal, you know. And gems for the saws, though they don't seem to find many of those. . . .

"Then Midwall, up-chasm, the other side of Nextdown, then Harvester's bridge, away down chasm where it bends, and last of all came Bottommost. Aunt Six says Bottommost is rebels and anarchists, but then she talks like that about a lot of things. I think it's Fishers, mostly, and Hunters, and some Crafters, and Banders and casteless types.'' She stopped to take a deep breath before continuing, gasping. Her ribs cut into her like knives. The arms around her tightened, then pillowed her more deeply.

"Tell me about castes. What are they?"

"Top caste is Bridgers. They're the ones who build the bridgetowns and maintain them and build the stairs and locate the water-bellies and all that. Then there are Crafters, who make things out of wood, mostly, though they use some metal, too. And Potters, and Porters, and Miners, and Teachers. And Harvesters. They train the slow-girules to harvest the nodules from the roots, and they harvest the wall moss, and fruits from the vines and all like that. And the Messengers. They have two jobs to do. We don't talk about one of them. The other—well, they fly. Not how you meant it when you asked. They put on wings, and then they jump out into the air when it rises, and they fly between the bridgetowns with messages or little things they can carry. Medicine, maybe. Or plans, to show the Bridger in the other city what's going on. Maintainers. They're the ones who take care of the Bridgers, feed them, clean their houses and all. Birders I already told you about. Then there are the Fishers, two kinds of those, one that fishes for floppers from the Fishers' roosts and those who drop their lines from Bottommost into the river down there, so far they can't even see it, and bring up fishes. And the Hunters who track game through the root mat. . . ." She stopped, exhausted.

"And you said something about casteless ones?"

Beedie sighed, weary beyond belief. "There are always some who don't fit in. Weavers—did I mention Weavers before?—who can't weave. Or Potters who can't do a pot. Or even Bridger children who get the down-dizzies when they look down. They may get adopted into some other caste, or they may ask to become Maintainers—some say Maintainers will take anybody, though I don't know if that's true—or they may just stay casteless. It's all right. No one hates them for it or anything. It's just that they don't have any caste house to live in or any special group to help them or take them in if they're sick or old or have a baby."

"Do people marry?"

"Oh, yes. In caste, usually, though not always. They say if you marry in caste, your kids will have the right aptitudes. That isn't true, by the way. Aunt Six says it never was true. She says having a child is like betting on a flopper's flight. They always go off in some direction you don't count on."

"What are caste houses?"

"Oh, like Bridgers House on Topbridge. Whenever there are enough of any one caste on one bridge, they build a caste house. Usually the elders of the caste live there, and any other caste members there's room for. One elder from each castehouse makes up the bridge council, though we usually just say 'the elders,' and they decide when to expand the bridgetown or build new stairs or pipe a new water-belly. I don't know what else to tell you. Except I hurt. Please let me stop talking."

"Just a moment more, sausage girl. What about clothing? Do the castes dress differently?"

Beedie could not understand the question. She tried to focus on the question and could not. Dress? How did they dress? "Like me," she whispered. "More or less. Trousers. Shirt. Only Bridgers wear belts like this. Harvesters wear leather aprons. Potters have very clean hands. Miners have dirty ones. . . . I can't . . . can't . . . " There was only a heavy darkness around her, a sense of vast movement, easy as flying, as though she were cushioned in some enormous, flying lap. Then there were voices.

"Are you her Aunt Six? The root she was working on . . . burning . . . the smoke . . . don't think she's seriously hurt . . . from Harvester's Bridge myself . . . just happened to see her as I was coming up the stairs . . . thank you, very kind of you. Yes, I would be glad to do that. Boneman, you say? In the yellow house next to Bridgers'? Never mind, ma'am, I'll find it. . . ."

Inside the darkness, Beedie felt herself amused. The bird/woman/person was leading Aunt Six about by the nose, pretending to be a Harvester from Harvester's Bridge. Beedie was enjoying it, even through the black curtain. It was very humorous. They had sent for the Boneman, to find out if anything was broken. So, she was home, home on Topbridge, in Aunt Six's new place. Now that she knew where she was, she could let the darkness have its own way. Though the voices went on, she stopped listening to them.

There seemed to be no next day, though there was a day after that. She swam lazily out of quiet into the light, feeling hands holding her head and the rim of a cup at her lips once more. This made her laugh, and she choked on the broth Aunt Six was trying to feed her, then couldn't explain what the laughter was about.

"Lucky you were, girl, that a doer-good came along just then. I was in little mood to trust any Harvester, as you can imagine, seeing what an arrogant bunch they are, as you well remember from just a few days ago. But this one, well, she told me someone had fired the root. . . .

"I sent the elders. They saw no sign of it, except the smell of smoke clinging. Greenwood smoke does cling, so they don't doubt the story at all, or the word of the doer-good, Mavin, her name is. I suppose you wouldn't remember that, being gone to all intents and meanings from that time to this." Aunt Six used her handkerchief, blowing a resounding blast. "A bad thing to take almost a whole family that way, your daddy and mother, all the uncles, then to try it with you, girl." The pillow was patted relentlessly into a hard, uncomfortable shape. "We can't imagine who. Who would it be?"

For some reason, all Beedie could think of was that phlegmy chuckle of old Slysaw Bander, the sneering eyes of Byle Bander, the two of them like as root hairs. Making mischief. But why? Why? Why would even a Bander do hurt to his own caste? What could he gain from it? How did he know I'd be going down there alone?

"Well, fool girl," a voice inside her head said, "He knew no such thing. He thought there'd be six or seven Bridgers, including a few elders." Then her head swam and accusations fled through it like birds through air. He must have thought he'd take six away with the root . . . the way he did before . . . the way he did before . . . the way he did before.

Gradually her mind slowed and quieted. Well, if it hadn't been for the doer-good, one Bridger would have fallen to the Bottom, but there could be no proof it had been planned or who by. Byle had probably been companied by five or six Bridgers all day, including at least one or two Chafers or Beeds. No proof. No proof, and all a waste, for the trap hadn't killed six, hadn't even killed one. Was that why Byle was so eager to get away from Bridgers House last night? To get someone else to set the fire he had planned to set himself?

Could she accuse him? Them? Byle hadn't had a chance to set that fire, so someone else had. Who? Slicksaw and her friends, while they were down there checking her measure? No. Too early to set it then, though they may well have made ready for it. And if so, was it a general thing, then? A conspiracy among all the Banders? To accomplish what? To kill Bridgers, evidently, but why?

Dizzy from the unanswerable questions in her mind, Beedie drifted off into gray nothing again, unable even to be curious about Mavin, the person/bird/woman who might be doing anything at all while Beedie slept.

She awoke to find a leather-aproned Harvester sitting in the window, the Harvester sipping at a cup while reading one of Aunt Six's books about religion; the steam from the tea curled over the lamp beside the bed. At first Beedie did not recognize the woman, but then something in the tilt of head said bird/person/creature, and Beedie smiled. "Good morning."

Mavin put down the tea cup and turned to pour another, offering it to the swaddled figure on the bed. "Say 'good evening,' sausage girl. You've spent a good time muffled up there, recovering from your wounds, I thought, but then, hearing your Aunty Six talk for a time, I figured it was only to escape the constant conversation."

Beedie tried to laugh, turning it into a gasp as her ribs creaked and knifed at her. "I don't think I'm better."

"Oh, yes. You've got a few cracked ribs where you hit the mainroot with the side of your ownself. The Boneman strapped them. He says they'll heal. You've got a nasty blue spot on your forehead spoiling your maidenly beauty. The Skin-woman put a foul-smelling poultice on that. Aside from that, there's not much wrong with you a few days lying about won't cure. Meantime, I've met the people at your Bridgers House and been thanked by them for saving you. There's been a good deal of climbing up and down as well, trying to figure out what set the root afire—or maybe *who* set it afire. Far as I can learn, no one knows for sure, though there seem to be whispered suspicions floating here and there. Your Bridger elder, Rootweaver, says I have a strange accent and must come from the fartherest end of Harvesters where no one talks in a civilized manner, but she was kind enough for all that."

"Rootweaver is a good person."

"True. She is such a good person I told her some of the things I had seen 'on my way up from Harvesters.' To which she replied by trading confidences, telling me that something seems to be eating the verticals of the bridgetowns. Killing them dead, so she says. Giving me a keen look while she told me, too, as though she thought I might have been eating them myself. Had you heard about that?"

"Something of the kind," murmured Beedie. "The Bridgers are very upset about it."

"Indeed? Well, I heard her out. Since then, I have waited for you to recover so that you can take me to see the greatest wonder of Topbridge."

"And what's that, Mavin doer-good?"

"Doer-good, am I? Well, perhaps I am. The wonder I speak of is the birdwoman, sausage girl. I'd rather visit her with someone discreet by my side. Someone who knows more than she says. That is, unless your praiseworthy silence results from inability to talk rather than discretion."

"Oh, I can talk," Beedie said, proving it. "But when there are strangenesses all about, better maybe to keep shut and wait until talk is needed. My father used to say that."

"Pity he didn't tell your Aunt Six. Why was she named Six, anyhow?"

"She was named Six because when she was a girl, she always insisted on carrying six spare straps for her spurs. Not four, nor five, but six. And if my father had tried to tell her anything, she wouldn't have listened.

She would have been too busy talking. And'' —she shifted uncomfortably— ''I have to go.''

''If you mean you have to *go*, the Boneman who looked at you said you could. Get up, I mean. Just take it easy, don't lift anything, don't bump yourself. Is there a privy in here?''

''Of course. Do you think we live like floppers?'' Beedie struggled out of the bed and across the room, feeling the cold boards on her feet with a sense of relief. Until that moment she had not been sure she could stand up. She left the privy door ajar, letting the heat from the bedroom warm all of her but her bottom, poised bare over the privy hole, nothing but air all the way to the Bottom and all the night winds of the chasm blowing on her. ''All the houses on all the bridges have privies. That's why we don't build bridges one under the other, and that's why we put roofs on the stairs.''

When she returned to the bed, Mavin handed her a piece of paper and a pen. ''Draw me a plan, girl. Looking end on, how are these bridges of yours arranged? How do we get from one to another supposing—as it would be wise for us to suppose—neither of us can fly?''

Beedie sipped at her tea, propped the paper against her knees and thought. Finally, she drew a little plan on the paper and handed it to Mavin. ''There. These are the ends of the bridges. There's a stair from Topbridge to Nextdown. There are two stairs from Nextdown; one on down to Midwall, another winding one across under Topbridge to Potter's. From Potter's there's a stair down to Miner's; and from Miner's, there's a stair up to Harvester's. Then, from Midwall, there's a stair down under Nextdown to Bottommost. There are rest places on that stair, and from Bottommost there's a long stair which leads along the Wall to mine entrances way below Miner's and then goes on and meets the Harvester's trail way below Harvester's. Some of these stairs are at the morning-light end, and some at the evening-light end of the bridgetowns, so it can be a long walk between Potter's and Topbridge. That's why we have messengers, if word needs to be carried quickly on wings. There's one hot spot right below us, off the edge of Topbridge."

"Hot spot?"

"Where the air rises, where the Messengers fly. Remember, I told you. There are other hot spots here and there, every bridge has at least one close by. There's a big one near Harvester's, around the corner of the chasm. No one knows what causes hot spots, though some of the old books say it's probably hot springs, water that comes out of the ground hot."

"And you've never been to any of these places?"

"I was born on Nextdown. And I came here. And that's all."

"Ah. Well, if I go journeying while I'm here, perhaps you'd like to go along? But first, you'll sleep some more and recover entirely. I hear your aunt coming. Time for me to get along to Harvesters House. . . ."

"They took you in then, at Harvesters House?" Beedie whispered.

"Why shouldn't they? I'm a Harvester, aren't I? I work well with the slow-girules, don't I? Besides, you can tell by my apron." And Mavin winked at her, making a droll face, strolling out of the room and away.

"A very pleasant doer-good," said Aunt Six. "Well spoken and kindly. You're a lucky girl, Beedie, to have had such a one climbing the stairs from Nextdown just at the time you needed help. And one not afraid of root climbing, either. What if it had been a Potter? Or a Miner? Not able to climb at all for the down-dizziness in their heads?"

"I'm very lucky," Beedie agreed, saying nothing at all more than that.

By afternoon of the third day from then, her ribs rebandaged by the Boneman, she was able to visit the Skin-woman who lived just off center lane, midchasm, by the market, in order to have another poultice put on her forehead. A train of Porters had brought in a great load of pots from Potter's bridge, and the Topbridgers were out in numbers, bargaining in a great gabble for cook pots and storage pots and soup bowls. Mavin and

THE FLIGHT OF MAVIN MANYSHAPED   39

Beedie walked among the stalls, half hearing it all, while they spoke of the birdwoman at Birders House.

"Of course they'll let you see her!" said Beedie. "As a messenger of the Boundless, she can be seen by anyone, for any person might be sent a message from the Boundless, and the Birders wouldn't know who."

"I've been in places they would tell you they did know," said Mavin in a dry voice. "And tell you what the message was, as extra."

"Why, how could anyone know? Would the Boundless give someone else my message to tell me? Silly. Of course not. If the Boundless had a message for me—which I am too unimportant to expect, mind you—it would give it directly to me, no fiddling about through other people."

Mavin laughed. "There are things about your society here that I like, girl. Your good sense about your religion is one of them."

Beedie shook her head in confusion. "If a religion doesn't make sense, what good is it? It has to make sense out of things to be helpful, and if it isn't helpful, who'd have it?"

"You'd be surprised, sausage girl. Very surprised. But here we are. Isn't this Birders?" They had stopped outside a tall, narrow house which reached up along the Wall, its corners and roof erupting in bird houses and cotes, its stairs littered with feathers and droppings, and with an open, latticed window just before them behind which a pale figure sat, smiling heedlessly and combing its long dark hair.

"Aree, aree," it sang. "The boundless sea, the white wave, the light wave, the soundless sea."

"Can we get closer?" asked Mavin in a strange, tense tone. "Where she can see us?"

"We can go in," Beedie answered. "We'll have to make an offering, but it won't be much. I'll tell them you have confusions and need to be blessed by the messenger."

"You do that, sausage girl. For it's true enough, come to think of it."

They went up the shallow stairs to the stoop and struck the bell with their hands, making it throb into the quiet of the street. A Birder came to the door, his blue gown and green stole making tall stripes of color against the dark interior. When Beedie explained, he beckoned them in.

"I'm Birder Brightfeather," he said, nodding to Beedie. "I know you, Bridger, and your parents before you. Though that was on Nextdown, and I am only recently come to Topbridge to help in the House here, for young Mercald was no longer able to handle the press of visitors. Will you offer to the Boundless before seeing the messenger?"

"If we may," answered Mavin easily, moving her hand from pocket to Birder's hand in one practiced gesture. The Birder seemed pleased at whatever it was he had been given.

"Of course. Go in. Stay behind the railing, please. She becomes frightened if people come too close. If you have a question, ask in a clear voice, and don't go on and on about it. The Boundless knows. We don't have to explain things to It. Then if there's an answer, the birdgirl will sing it. Or perhaps not. The Boundless does not always choose to answer, but then you know that." The Birder waved them into the room, through heavy drapes that shut away the rest of the House. They found themselves behind a waist-high barrier, the birdgirl seated before them, half turned away as she peered out through the lattice at the street, still singing as she combed her hair.

"No sorrow, tomorrow, tomorrow go free, to high flight, to sky flight, the boundless sea."

"Handbright," said Mavin, in a husky whisper. "Handbright. It's Mavin."

"Aree, aree," sang the birdgirl, slowly turning her head so that she could see them where they stood. She was dressed in a soft green robe, the color of the noonglow, with ribbons of blue and silver in her hair. Her face was bony, narrow, like the face of a bird. She looked like something out of the old tales, thought

Beedie, something remote and marvelously beautiful, too wonderful to be human. And yet, this Mavin spoke to her. . . .

"Handbright. Sister. See, it's Mavin. Come all the way from the lands of the True Game, all the great way from Danderbat Keep, from Schlaizy Noithn, from cliffbound Landizot and the marshy meadows of Mip, over the boundless sea to find you. It's been more than fifteen years, Handbright, and I was only fifteen when you saw me last."

"No sorrow, no sorrow, the soundless sea," sang the birdgirl, her eyes passing across them as though they did not exist. "Aree, aree." She stood up and moved about the room behind the railing, around her chair, half dancing, her feet making little patterns on the floor. Then she sat back down, but not before Mavin had seen the way the soft gown fell around her figure, no longer as painfully thin as it had been when Mavin had seen her last, no longer slender at all. Her belly bulged hugely above the thin legs.

"Ah," said Mavin, in a hurt tone. "So that's the way of it. Too late for you, Handbright. So late." She stood in a reverie, seeing in her head the great white bird, plumes floating from its wings and tail, as it dived from the tower of Danderbat Keep, as its wings caught the wind and it beat itself upward into the blue, the high blue; a color which these people of the chasm never saw, preserved only in these ribbons, in the ritual garments of their Birders. She saw herself, pursuing, asking here, there, high on the bounding cliffs of Schlaizy Noithn; among the seashore cities of fishermen who wore fishskin trousers and oiled ringlets; in Landizot, the childless town; high in the marshy mountain lands near Breem; among the boats of the hunter fleet which never came to land but plied from Summer Sea to Winter Sea, its children born to the creak of wood and the rattle of sheets; along the desert shore of this other land beyond the Western Sea, where there were no Games nor Gamesmen, coming at last to this people living pale and deep, beyond the light of the fructifying sun; fifteen years spent in searching, asking, following. "Well, I have found you at last, sister," she said to herself. "And your face is as peaceful as a candle flame in still air, burning with its own heat, consuming itself quietly, caring not. You sing and your voice is happy. You dance, and your feet are shod in silk. Oh, Handbright, why do I need to weep for you?"

She turned to take Beedie by the arm, her strong hands making pits in the girl's flesh so that she gasped. "Sorry, sausage girl. It is a sad thing to come too late. Ah well, let's go back to your place, my dear, and drink something warming. I feel all cold, like all the chasm night winds were blowing through me."

"What is it, Mavin? Why are you so upset? Do you know her? Is she truly your sister?"

"She is truly my sister, girl. Truly as ever was. I was fifteen when she left, when I told her to leave, but she is my sister, my Shifter sister, mad as any madman I have ever seen, and pregnant as any mother has ever been. And if I understand your religion, my dear, and the respect that would be due to a messenger of the Boundless, the fact that my sister will bear now—though she did not bear in years past, to her sorrow—bodes ill for the Birders. And, sausage girl, from what I have seen traveling the width of the world for fifteen years, when a thing bodes ill for the religion of a place, trouble follows, and anarchy and rebellion and terror." Her voice rang like a warning bell, insistant and troubling.

Beedie trembled at her tone. "Oh . . . surely, surely it is not such a great thing. . . ."

"Perhaps not. We will hope so. But I think best to consider it, nonetheless. There is time to be tricksy, child, and best to have plans made before needs must." She smiled and laid a hand gently on the girl's shoulder. Strange, to have come so far and made such an odd alliance at the end of it all. "Tush. Don't frown. We will think on it together." And she squeezed Beedie's shoulder in a gesture which, had she known it, was one Beedie's father had once used and thus won the girl to her as no words could have done.

Chapter 3

Trouble came more quickly than Mavin had foreseen, more quickly than Beedie would have thought possible. It was the following morning that they left Beedie's house on their way to take a breakfast cup of tea at one of the ubiquitous stalls, when they saw a Birder—not a person they would have recognized except for her robes—fleeing with loud cries of alarm from a group of youngsters intent upon doing her some immediate harm. The expressions on their snarling faces left no doubt, and when Mavin and Beedie came among them like vengeful furies, pushing and tossing them about like so many woodchips, they responded with self-righteous howls. "They're blasphemers, the Birders. . . . They've blasphemed the Boundless . . . else she's no messenger . . . need to be taught a lesson. . . . My dad says they should be whipped." Indeed, one of the leaders of the child pack had a whip with him.

"And who are you to be judge of the Birders? And what have they done that is blasphemous?" Mavin demanded in a voice of thunder, drawing a good deal of

attention from passers-by, including the parents of
some of those cowering before her who shifted uneasily
from foot to foot wondering how far they might go in
interfering with this angry stranger. Beedie, throwing
quick looks around, was horrified to note that a good
part of the child pack was made up of Bridgers—Bander
whelps—as good a guarantee as any that they might go
about their evil business without being called to account
for it.

"My dad says . . . no fit judges for us anymore
. . . did a bad thing. . . . Either that or she's no messenger. . . ."

Mavin seized the speaker and shook him. "Before
you decide to run a mob behind you, boy, better wonder
what vengeance the Birders might take if you are wrong!
Have you thought what may come from the Boundless
as messenger . . . to you . . . in the dark night . . . with
no mob about to protect you?" Her voice shivered like a
maddened thing; wild-eyed, her hands shook as though
in terror. The boy began to tremble in her grasp, eyes
widening, until he broke from her to fall on his knees,
bellowing his fear. Beedie was amazed. Anyone within
reach of Mavin's voice could feel the terror, the awful-
ness of that messenger who might come. The boy took
his fear from her pretended feeling, cowering away as
though she had threatened him with immediate destruc-
tion. The adults gathered about were no less affected,
and several of the young ones were hauled away by
parents abruptly concerned for their own welfare
though they had been egging the children on until that
moment.

The other whelps ran off down an alley, yelping as
they went. Mavin spun the boy with the whip around,
kicking him off after them, and wiped her hands in
disgust. The Birder, who had paused at the turn of the
street, returned to thank them.

"This riot and attack is all up and down the chasm,"
she said, still breathless. "I came to warn the Birders
House here on Topbridge, for our house on Nextdown
is virtually under seige, and no sooner set foot upon the

street than that gang attacked me. They were set on me! I saw their fathers or older brothers urging them on from a teahouse door.''

"You'd best let us take you to the Birders House," ventured Beedie.

"You'd best stay there when you arrive," Mavin instructed her. "There is a kind of animal frenzy can be whipped up sometimes among fools and children, often using religion as an excuse for it. When it happens, it is wise to be elsewhere.''

They escorted the Birder to the House, much aware of gossiping groups falling silent as they passed, much aware of eyes at windows, of chunks of root thrown at them and easily fended off by either Mavin or Beedie, who walked virtually back to back in protection of the robed woman. Once at the Birders House, Mavin asked for Mercald and learned that he had been sent to the far end of Topbridge to gather the shed plumes of gongbirds, used by the Birders in their rituals. "He will return momentarily," dithered Brightfeather. "I told him to set his robes aside and go. With all this confusion and the violence outside, I wanted some time alone, to think. I don't understand what is happening.''

"Violence outside?" The newly arrived Birder was peering from the window. They could see no sign of trouble, but the Birder assured them there were small groups of ill doers lurking just out of sight.

This was confirmed as they came from the house after the visit. They encountered a group of Topbridgers skulking just inside an alleyway, keeping watch upon the Birders House.

"There's some. Ask'm," muttered one of the loiterers, thrusting another out of the alley at them. "Ask'm whether it's true. She's puff-belly, right? Ask'm.''

" 'Ja see the birdgirl?" panted the thrustee. "There's some saying she's swole. Been havin' at her, those Birders, some say. Mercald's had atter. 'Ja see her?''

Beedie started to say something indignant, but the pressure from Mavin's hand stayed her. "Oh, I have indeed," said Mavin. "There are three schools of thought, good people, among those from Harvesters. One school teaches that the birdwoman was pregnant when she came to us, but a long pregnancy of a strange, messengerial kind, and that it is the desire of the Boundless that we foster her child. Then another opinion teaches that she became pregnant sometime after she came, and that it will be her child who carries the message from the Boundless. And a third opinion teaches that it was the intention of the Boundless she become pregnant, but only to illustrate that the holy and the human are of like kind. Be wary, people, for we do not yet know the truth of this, and it would not be wise to anger the Boundless." And Mavin fixed them with eyes which seemed to glow with a mysterious fire even as she, herself, seemed to grow taller and more marvelous. It was less overt than the technique she had used upon the youths, but it worked no less well. The men stopped muttering and merely gazed at her, their mouths gaped wide like that of the puffed fish lantern above them, working over the phrases they had rehearsed, now impotent to arouse themselves with their litany of hate. When they had thus gazed for a little time, Mavin brought them back to the present. "You might ask," she said in a voice of portentous meaning, "among your acquaintances, which of these theories they subscribe to. Which, for example, do you yourselves believe? You may be held accountable for your belief."

There was a muttering, a scuttling, and the two of them were quite suddenly alone.

"I'd love to know where you learned to do that with your voice," Beedie said. "Where you learned to do that trick you did earlier, with the boys, and this one, with these fellows. It's in your eyes and your face. Suddenly they forget what they were about to do. They get real worried about themselves. You'd been planning that, hadn't you? You were ready for those brats, for these folk. You knew they'd been put up to that talk." Then, in a voice of sudden revulsion, "Someone's been stirring a vat of chasm air about the Birders."

"Oh, assuredly they'd been put up to it. But I've given them other matter to chatter on. The interesting part of it is, who did it? Who blamed the Birders right off? Who blamed Mercald? And why?"

"To prevent the Birder caste being raised," she answered, sure of it. "Though why it should matter to them, I cannot tell."

"Ah. Tell me, Beedie, what is this lantern we stand under, and why have I not seen them before?"

"Because there aren't many of them, Mavin," she replied, confused at this change of subject. "Most of them are very old and rare. They come from the Bottomlands. Fishers catch them sometimes. They glow, you see. The Fishers take out the insides and blow up the skin, then when it's dark, the skin glows. The Fishers say there are many glowing things deep in the chasm. These are about the only ones they can catch, however."

"Interesting. It glows. You know, root dangler, the bottom of your chasm is a wonderful and mysterious place, wonderfully attractive to such an adventurer as I."

"I told you before, it's dangerous down there, Mavin."

"I think it's going to get dangerous up here, girl. Now use your head to help me think. Why would anyone not want another caste raised up? You told me that the Bridgers were top caste. What does that mean in simple language?"

"Simple language is all I have," she said with some dignity. "It means the eldest Bridger is the head of the chasm council."

"That's all?"

"That's enough. Head of the chasm council can do almost anything. The head can decide to build a new bridgetown. Or send off an expedition. Or assess new taxes. Or get up an army, not that we've ever needed one since we came down from Firstbridge. Or assign duties to a caste, or take duties away."

"All by himself, he can do this?"

"Or herself, yes. Not that they do go off all on their own like that. Mostly they're quiet kinds who do a lot of talk before they decide anything. You've met Rootweaver. Likely, she'll be next head of council. Her cousin, old Quickaxe, is head now, but he's getting very feeble. Either he'll resign or he'll die or become so ill the council will declare him honorably dis-casted."

"And how old is Rootweaver?"

"How old? I haven't any idea."

"How old is—oh, the Bander from Nextdown, Byle's daddy, Slysaw?"

"Almost as old as Rootweaver, I suppose."

"So, if Rootweaver died, and maybe a few others younger than she but older than Slysaw, who would be the eldest Bridger in the whole chasm? Hmmm, girl?" Mavin paused, smiling dangerously while Beedie considered this. "And you think the Bottom would be dangerous, do you? I'll tell you, nothing is so dangerous as ambition in a man who cares not who stands in his way."

"Slysaw Bander? Oh, the day he became eldest Bridger is the day we would all change caste. It's disgusting! No one would have him."

"Oh, girl, girl. So speaks the naivete of youth. Why, I have seen such tyrants as you would not believe cheered and carried on the shoulders of their countrymen in that same frenzy the boys were whipped up to this morning. I'll wager you, girl, you'll find some in the teashops today who are talking of Slysaw, telling of his generosity, and what good ideas he has, and how much things would be improved if he were eldest Bridger. I'll wager there are casteless ones and bitty members of this caste and that one, including more than a few Bridgers, probably, all with sudden coin in their pockets and free time to talk endlessly, all talking of Slysaw Bridger and what a fine fellow he is."

Beedie, who had learned something about Mavin in the last day or so, said, "You'll wager what they're saying in the teashops because you've heard them."

"Right first time, sausage girl. There seem to be

many visitors from Nextdown in your bridgetown, more than I can figure why they've come. They seem to have no business but talk. But they are talking, endlessly.''

"But why—I still can't figure why, Mavin. If old Slysaw lit the fire that killed my daddy and mother, well, I'll believe anything of him including he's a devil. But I can't figure why.''

"Because there's power to be had, girl. I'll tell you a tale, now. Suppose these talkers go to the teashop and go on with their talking, fuming and blowing, saying how terrible it is what the Birders have done, maybe how terrible it is what the birdgirl has done. . . .''

"Maybe saying she's no messenger from the Boundless at all?''

"Words like that. The sense of it doesn't matter much, so long as the sound is full of indignation and fire. So, they talk and talk, getting fierier and fierier, until at last some of them go to set matters right. How will they do that?''

"Bring Mercald and the Birders up before the judges.''

"Ah. But it's Birders *are* your judges, girl, and Birders they claim are doing evil. So, what is it they'll cry then?''

"They'll cry the judges are corrupt; they'll say they'll have to do justice on their own. . . .''

"Right again. And their justice will mean killing someone, maybe Mercald, maybe half a dozen other Birders or all of them, maybe the birdwoman. . . .''

"Which you won't . . . you can't let happen,'' whispered Beedie, beginning to understand for the first time what a tricksy person sat beside her.

"Which I won't let happen. Meantime, there's confusion and threats and maybe a few little riots. You've got no kind of strong arms in this chasm except the Bridgers themselves, perhaps, and you'll have to forgive my saying it, girl, but they seem half asleep to what's going on.''

"They've never—had to . . .''

"That's obvious. Well then, with all the confusion,

this one and that one could get killed. And wouldn't it be strange if among those killed were a number of elderly Bridgers? And at the end of it strange that Slysaw Bridger would happen to be eldest Bridger in the chasm and thus head of council. And in the meantime, of course, everyone too upset and confused to wonder who fired the mainroot you almost died on."

"How could any Bridger do such a thing?" she demanded, white around her eyes, mouth drawn up into an expression of horror and distaste. "Even a Bander shouldn't be able to think of such things. I wouldn't have thought that, ever."

"Which is what he counts upon, sausage girl. He counts on no one believing ill of a fellow caste member. He counts on being able to sow distrust without being suspected of it or blamed for it. He cares nothing for the religion, so does not fear to meddle with it. He's no believer, that one. Else he wouldn't have trifled with a messenger of the Boundless."

"I thought she wasn't—that she was just your sister, Mavin. I'm all confused. . . ."

"She's my sister right enough. But who's to say what messengers the Boundless sends? Why not my sister?"

"Why not you?" asked Beedie, whispering.

"Ah. Why not me, indeed. Well, then, this messenger needs a word with your lady Rootweaver, and it's up to you to arrange it, Beedie. Arrange it quietly, and in a way no one will wonder at, for I've things to tell her and her fellows, things to ask of her as well, and I want no prying ears while I'm doing it."

"You're not going to tell them that you . . . "

"I'm not going to tell them anything except what any Harvester might have overheard, in a teashop, say. Or at a procession. And if you're asked, girl, you know nothing about anything at all except that I saved your skin on the mainroot one day as I came climbing up from Nextdown. That way, whatever I say, you know nothing about it."

"I could help you," Beedie pleaded.

"Not yet. Come necessary time, then yes, but not now. Just go along to Rootweaver, child, and give me the space of a few minutes to think what I'm going to say to her." She turned to lean on the railing of the bridge, leaning out a little to let the updraft bathe her face in its damp, cool movement, full of the scent of strange growths and pungent herbs. Behind her, Beedie dithered from foot to foot for a moment before moving off purposefully toward the Bridgers House. Mavin put her face in her hands, letting herself feel doubt and dismay she would not show before the girl. She felt disaster stirring in every breath of air and was not completely sure she could save Handbright, either her life or the life she carried.

Far out on a Fishing bridge, which jutted from the mainbridge like a broken branch, she saw a Fisher blowing into his flopper call, making a low honking that echoed back from some distant protrusion of the wall. He put the call away to stand quiet, flicking his line above his head in long, curled figures as a chorus of honks came from inside the root wall. Too quickly for the eyes to follow, a flopper dropped from the root wall, planing across the chasm on the skin stretched from forelegs to backlegs, folding up from time to time to drop like a plummet in the intermittent flops which gave the creatures their name, then opening the stretched skin to glide over the chasm depths once more. The Fisher's line snapped out, the weighted hooks at the end of it gleaming in the evening light, missing the flopper by only an arm's breadth. Another flopper fell from the root wall, and this time the hook caught it firmly through the skin of its glider planes. The flopper honked, a long, dismal hoot into the dusk, and the Fisher began hauling in against the struggling weight.

"Caught," breathed Mavin. "Handbright, you dropped out of Danderbat Keep on wings, on wings, girl, and you've been hooked here in this chasm, the hook set so deep I may never get you loose." She fell silent, thinking about the technique she had used in diverting the mob of boys, the one she had used on the men. When had she learned to do that? And how? It seemed a long time past, a great distance gone.

There had been a town, she remembered, along the coast north of Schlaizy Noithn, separated from the world of the True Game by high cliffs and from the sea by a curving wall of stone around a placid harbor, such a wall as might have resulted from the innundation of some ancient fire mountain. The people of that town had called it Landizot. She came there seeking Handbright and the company of humankind but found a people hesitant and wary, uneasy with strangers and as uneasy among themselves. Yes, they said, there had been a white bird high upon the cliffs—those they called the dawn wall—earlier in the year. The young people had pursued it there, setting nets for it, mimicking its call in an effort to entice it down, but the bird had avoided them easily, circling high above the cliffs in the light of early morning or at dusk, when it gleamed like silver against the mute purple of the sky.

When had it last been seen, Mavin asked, only to be confronted with shrugs and disclaimers. The children had not been allowed to play outside lately, she was told. Not for some time. So they had not seen it. No one went outside much, certainly not alone at dusk, and the bird had always avoided groups. Perhaps it was still there. Perhaps not.

Mavin decided to stay a while and look around for herself. When she asked why people no longer ventured from their locked houses with the barred windows and doors, she did so in that flat, incurious voice she had learned to use in her travels, one which evinced a polite interest but without sufficient avidity to stir concern among casual talkers.

"Because," she was told, "they have released the Wolf." The person who told her this glanced about with frightened eyes and would say nothing else. Stepping away from this encounter, Mavin looked into the faces of others to find both fear and anger there.

When she enquired, they said they were not Gamesmen, that they repudiated Gaming as a wicked thing, if indeed even a tenth of what was said about it was true. They did not want to be thought of as pawns, however. They were an ancient people, they said, with their own ways of doing things. Mavin smiled her traveler's smile, said nothing about herself at all, but made a habit of sitting about in the commons room of her inn at night, listening.

At first there was little conversation. The people who came there at the supper hour were the lone men and women of the town, those without family. They ate silently, drank silently, and many of them left once they had eaten so that the room was almost empty by dusk. As the evenings wore on, however, a few truculent men and a leathery woman or two found their way to the inn to drink wine or beer and huddle in the warmth of the fire. Mavin, with a laconic utterance, offered to buy drink for those present. Later in each evening that courtesy was returned. On the third or fourth night she sat near one old couple who, when the wine had bubbled its way through to their tongues, began to talk, not much, but some.

"Stranger woman, you'll stay here in the place after dark at night, won't you?"

"I'd planned on it," said Mavin.

"Don't go out at night. You're not young as most of the girls or children who've been et, but you're female, and the good Guardians witness the Wolf has eaten older."

Mavin thought about this for a while, not wanting to seem too interested. "Is that the same Wolf I'm told was let out?"

"There is no other," said the old woman. "And thanks be to all the Guardians for that."

"What had he done, to be locked up?" She kept her voice calm, almost uninterested, so the woman would not feel it would be troublesome to tell her.

"Killed a woman. Drank her blood. And after crying remorse and swearing he would not do such a thing again."

"Oh," said Mavin. "Then the Wolf had been locked up before."

"Aye," responded the oldster. "Twice, now. First time he was young, the Wolf. There were those said young ones find society troublesome and strange, so it wouldn't do to set him down too hard for it. So, that time they locked him up for a season, no time at all."

"And the second time?" Mavin prompted.

"Well, second time they locked him for a full year. A full year. That's a weary long time, they said. A full year. Tssh. Seems years go past like autumn birds to me, all in a flock, so fast you can't see them clear. But then, I'm old."

"So they've let him out?" Mavin prompted again.

"Well, the time they set for him was done. Since it's done, they let him out."

"The time seems very short. For one who ate a young woman and drank her blood."

The oldsters shifted uncomfortably on their chairs, and Mavin changed the subject. Still, she thought a year seemed a very short time indeed.

When all had gone save the innkeeper himself, she yawned her way past him on the stairs, remarking as she did so that the two oldsters had seemed upset at the short confinement of the Wolf.

"Those two," snorted the innkeeper, wiping his hands on his protruding, apron-covered belly. "They're among those howling loudest at the cost of it. Wolf isn't eating them, they say, so why should they want to pay for it?"

"Pay for what?" asked Mavin, unable to keep the curiosity out of her voice.

"Pay to keep him locked up, woman! You think it comes free?" And he snorted his way to his rest, shaking his head up all three flights of stairs, calling back down to her, "Tell truth, though. They've got nothing. It's all they can do to keep their own hovel warm without buying firewood for the Wolf."

Next day Mavin had strolled about the town, seeking among the children for any who might have seen the white bird. In her walk she passed the prison lately vacated by the Wolf. Though it looked like a dreary place, it had every comfort in it of warmth and food and drink and soft mattresses and a shelf of amusements and a place to run in for exercise. Seeing it, Mavin well knew it had cost treasure to keep it, for the wood to burn to warm for it for a winter alone would have cost many days' labor, and the food many days' labor more, to say nothing of the guards who would have been needed night and day.

A number of children claimed to have seen the bird. One lovely girl of about ten years believed it had flown away south. Her name was Janine, called Janny, and she tagged after Mavin for the better part of five days, talking of the bird, the dawn cliffs, of life and the ways of the world while begging for stories of that world in return. The child was artless and delightful, full of ready laughter. Though Mavin had learned all there was to learn about the white bird, she put off her travels for a time out of simple joy in the girl's company.

One night there was a new face at the inn, a local preacher of Landizot, one Pastor Kyndle, whose house had been burned down by someone or something and would live at the inn while it was being rebuilt. Seeing Mavin was a stranger to the place, he set about making himself pleasant with the intent of converting her to the faith of Landizot and the Guardians. Talk turned, as it often did, to the Wolf.

"Why didn't they kill the Wolf when they caught him?" she asked. "Or, if they won't do that, why don't they lock the Wolf in a cage of iron here in the village square and let him shiver when the nights are cold. Surely he would be no colder than the corpses of the young women and children who lie in your burying ground?"

The pastor was much disturbed at this. "It would be cruel," he said. "Cruel to treat a person so. We are *good* people. Not cruel people."

Mavin shook her head, but withheld any judgment. If there was anything she had learned in long travels here and there, it was that to most people in the world, every unfamiliar thing was considered unacceptably strange. She told herself she was undoubtedly as odd to them as they were to her, and let the matter go. She determined to continue her search for Handbright as soon as the weather warmed only a little. She stopped asking questions and settled into the place, merely waiting for the snows to melt.

But before the thaw came a wicked murder of a young girl child of the town. Her body was found at the edge of the woods, dragged there by something. There was blood on the snow, and tracks of someone who had struck her down and drunk her blood. The tracks disappeared in the hard-packed ice of the road, however, and could lead them nowhere. The little girl was Janny, and Mavin learned of it with a cold horror which turned to fury.

That night in the inn were only murmurings and sideways glances, and more than once Mavin heard this one or that one speaking the Wolf's name. She expected before the night was over to hear he had been taken into confinement once more, but such was not to be.

He had not left the tavern, they said. He had been in his room drinking with his friends. All night. Never alone, not for a minute. His friends swore to it—Hog Boarfast, and Huggle, the brickmaker's son, and Hot Haialy, the son of Widow Haialy who had beggared herself trying to help him out of one scrape after the other.

"With them all night, was he?" murmured Mavin, controlling her voice with some difficulty.

"So they say."

"Trustworthy men, these? Those who say the Wolf was with them?"

"Well . . . there's no proof not. I mean, who's to say not?"

"Where did they get to know one another? The Wolf and these friends of his?"

"By the hundred devils, traveler, how would I know? All of 'em were born and raised here. Wolf, now, he came more lately, but I don't keep track of him. Most likely they got to know one another while they were locked up—all of 'em have been at one time or another. Or over the wine jugs at the Spotted Fustigar.''

Mavin smiled a narrow smile and bought the man a drink. As days wore on, her fury did not abate. In a few days was another killing, and once more the three friends of the Wolf swore he had been with them in the tavern. Mavin had known this child, too—one like Janine, trusting, joyous, kind. The next day Mavin left town with some noise about it, saying she would return in a few day's time. Instead, she returned that evening in the guise of a wastrel youth who took a room at the Spotted Fustigar and bought drinks for all and sundry in the tavern. It took no time at all to be introduced to Hog, Huggle, and Hot, and when one met them, one met the Wolf.

He had yellow eyes, and a slanted smile. His eyebrows met over his nose, and he had a feral, soft-voiced charm which had the new young barmaid, who was scarcely more than a child herself, bemused and troubled before the evening was half done. Hog, Huggle, and Hot were youths of a type; one fat, one meaty, one lean, but all as ignorant of the world as day-old bunwits and covering that ignorance with noise. Mavin set herself to be agreeable—which no others in that place did—and before much had been drunk or more than a dozen disgusting stories told, Mavin, too, was among the Wolf's close friends. During the fits of lewd laughter, Mavin had looked deep into the faces of the other friends of the Wolf to see the mindless excitements stirring there, gleaming in their eyes like rotten fish on tide flats.

Each day that passed there were fewer people on the streets, each night was closer locked and tighter fastened. The childlike barmaid seemed to stop breathing when the Wolf came near, yet she could not stay far from him. She was always within reach of his hands, always seeking his eyes with an open-lipped fascination. Mavin, watching, made angry, silent comments to herself.

Came an evening the Wolf said, "I'll be here all night tomorrow, won't I, Huddle?" He giggled, a high-pitched whine of excitement. "It's time for a good boozer, eh, Hog, all us good friends together, up in my rooms. Time for hooraw till the cock tries to get up and can't!"

There was a shifting, eager laughter among the three, in which Mavin joined beneath Wolf's speculative eyes. "I'll be back for it," she gasped from her wastrel's face, pretending drunken amusement. "Got to go to Fanthooly in the morning, but I'll be back before dark."

"What's of such interest in Fanthooly?" drawled the Wolf, his suspicious eyes burning in his face so that they seemed to whirl like little wheels of fire. The others hung on his words, ready to laugh or strike, as he bid.

"Old aunty with money, Wolf. Every year, money left me by dead daddy. She has it ready for me, same time, every year, in Fanthooly." Mavin appeared too drunk to have invented this, and the four had been drinking at Mavin's expense for some days, so they laughed and believed, saying they would save a drink for him. Mavin, in her wastrel guise, set off in the direction of Fanthooly the following morning.

Only to return, under cover of the forest, entering Landizot once more at the first fall of dark.

She went to the alleyway behind the Spotted Fustigar. There was a door into an areaway in which the trash could be dumped, and if Mavin had read the signs aright, it was there the young barmaid would come, charmed as a bird is said to be charmed by a serpent. And she came, sneaking out without a lantern, wrapped tight in a thick shawl, face both eager and apprehensive. Mavin took hold of her from behind in a hard, unpleasant way which would leave her with a headache but do no other damage, then dragged her unconscious form into the stables. Shortly, the same shawl was in the areaway once more, wrapped around someone else.

The Wolf came there, as she had known he would.

He did not waste his time with words or kisses. The knife was in his hand when he took hold of her, and it stayed in his hand when she took hold of him.

Mavin had been curious about his eyes. She wanted to know if they would glow in that way if he were afraid, if he were terrified, if he knew he was about to die. She found he could not believe in his own death—later she thought that might be why the deaths of so many others had meant nothing to him—so, she tried her voice to see whether she could convince him. After a time she caught the knack of it; by the end of it, the Wolf was truly convinced.

It was Hog who found him later that night, lying in his blood, yellow eyes filmed over and tongue protruding from between his slanted lips, the knife still in his hand.

In the morning, Mavin returned to Landizot as herself, full of tsks and oh-my's at the Wolf's sad end. She was questioned about the Wolf's death, as were others, but there was no proof. A stranger young man had been among the Wolf's friends, and it was thought he might have committed the deed except that he had been seen leaving for Fanthooly earlier that day.

As far as Mavin was concerned, the matter was done with. She could not restore Janine to life, but no other Janine would die. She was no longer angry, and she felt she had repaid whatever hospitality had been shown her.

One of the officials of the town came to Mavin afterward, however, with many suspicious questions and lectures on morality. Mavin was sure Pastor Kyndle had cast suspicion on her because of her views. She was sure of it when the official talked on and on about the Wolf's demise.

"Why?" he asked, attacking her, apropos of nothing.

"Why was he killed? Why, I suppose because he made a habit of killing others. Surely no one except himself expected him to be allowed to do it forever?" Mavin asked it as a question, but it seemed only to agitate the man.

"We had no proof he was still killing. Perhaps it was

someone else who was killing the women.''

"Perhaps," Mavin shrugged.

"Whoever killed the Wolf had no right . . . " the official began.

"Explain to me again," asked Mavin, "because I am a stranger. Why was it you could not subject the Wolf to the cruelty of a cage? Why did you not simply kill him the first time? You had proof then."

"Because he is—was human."

"Indeed? How did you know that?"

"Why, because his mother was human, and his father."

"Ah. And is that all humanity is? To be born from others who appear human? What does it mean, humanity?"

"It means," said the official with some asperity, "that he was born in the ordinary way and therefore had a soul. We cannot subject someone with a soul to cruel or horrible punishment."

"Ah," said Mavin, cocking her head in a way she knew to be particularly infuriating. "And the young women and children he killed? Did they also have souls?"

"Of course."

"And by Landizot's failure to restrain the Wolf, were they not cruelly treated and horribly punished? Was your town not guilty, therefore, of a grievous and very cruel punishment of the innocent? Ah—I see from your face I have missed some subtlety and fail to understand. Forgive me. I am a stranger and quite stupid." By this time she was also very angry, for the man had begun to bluster and threaten.

Though she had intended to leave the town at the first thaw, the thaw came while she lingered near Landizot in a cave high upon the dawn wall. The town had acquired a new Wolf. She spent the next season and a half stealing all the children of that town up to the age of ten or so and carrying them away, far away, to be fostered in desmenes beyond the mountains, over the chasms in the world of the True Game. The people of Landizot were much upset, but they had no proof, so could do nothing. When she had taken all the children to the least, newest baby, she enticed the inhabitants of the town out onto the beach, then burned the town behind them, leaving them weeping upon the shore.

She appeared to them then, only that once, in the guise of a terrible, wonderful beast, using the voice she had learned to use in the alley with the Wolf. "I will teach you my teaching, people," she roared at them. "No man gets a man's soul by birth alone. That which behaves like a Wolf is a Wolf, no matter who bore him. I have judged you all and found you guilty of foolishness, and this is the punishment, that you shall walk shelterless and childless until you learn better sense."

After which she left them.

She remembered this now as she stood beside the rail on Topbridge, roiling with the same kind of fury she had felt in Landizot, seething with a hundred ideas for intervention, wondering how much of it she could justify to herself. She had been young then, only eighteen. Even so, she had not been able to excuse having been judge and executioner as a youthful prank. It had not been without consequence. There were still nights when she wakened from a dream of the Landizot children mourning that they would not see their people again. And yet, even so, she still believed they were better in the lands of the True Game, whatever might befall them, than in the town of Landizot beside the ancient sea. At least in the lands of the True Game, people who gambled with women's lives did not claim to do it out of morality.

In the last several days she had stood in the Birders House more than once, hands resting upon the railing, listening to the voice of Handbright singing. There was no sorrow in that voice, and it was that as much as anything that had stayed Mavin from precipitous action. She had not yet seen Mercald. With Beedie off talking to the Bridger elders, perhaps now would be time to do it, though Mavin dreaded it. When she thought of Handbright and her pregnancy, she could

think of it only in terms of the abuses of Danderbat
Keep, and her anger envisioned what the man would
look like and how she would hate him.

In which she was wrong.

He was slight and pale as a boy, soft-spoken, mild as
mother's milk, timidly diffident, stuttering, his fingers
perpetually catching to twist on one another as a baby's
do in the crib. He was dressed in the blue and green of
the Birders, but on him it looked like festival dress, a
child got up in costume, at once proud and shy, and his
smile was a child's smile, abruptly radiant. In that instant, Mavin knew she had been wrong and in what
degree, for Mercald was like Mertyn, Handbright's
younger brother and her own, Mertyn who had held
Handbright in Danderbat Keep out of love long after
she should have left it out of pain.

"You're Beedie's doer-good," he said breathlessly,
holding out his hand, trembling in his desire to thank
her. "We have all blessed the Boundless that you were
there when needed to help her and save her."

"Yes," she said, changing her mind suddenly, as she
sometimes did. "I am Beedie's doer-good. I am also the
sister of the person you call the birdwoman. Her name is
Handbright."

His skin turned white, then flushed, the hot blush
mounting from his neck across his face to the tips of his
ears, onto his scalp to glow through his light hair like
the ruddy glow of a lamp. His hands went to his mouth,
trembling there, and his eyes filled with tears. Mavin
found herself wondering who had beat him as a child,
why he felt this fear, finally deciding that it was merely
an excess of conscience, an over-sufficiency of religious
sensibility.

"Come," she said harshly. "If I can forgive you,
surely the Boundless will do no less."

"Forgive . . . " he muttered in a pathetic attempt at
dissimulation. "What . . . is there to forgive?"

"She's pregnant, Birder. Having seen you, I can tell
you how and why and even when, mostlike. You didn't

plan it, did you? Didn't even think of it. It was just that she had been here for some time, sometime weeping, and you held her, and then—well, whist, it happens. She didn't mind at all, no doubt.''

"No," he wept. "I prayed forgiveness of the Boundless, so to have treated his messenger with such disrespect, but then as time went by, I thought perhaps it had been intended. Oh, but I am soiled beyond all cleansing. . . .''

"Nonsense," said Mavin impatiently. "You are silly beyond all belief, but that is your sole sin I am aware of, young man. I have no doubt that even now you do not know what trouble this will cause."

"I will be disgraced," he said in a sorrowful voice. "And it is right I should be."

"If that were all, we could possibly bear it with equanimity," she said, "but there is more to it than that. There is a deal of riot and murder involved. Well. I have seen you, Mercald. Having seen you, I may not become angry with you, for I do not become angry with children."

He flushed again, this time offended.

"Ah," she thought. "So he is capable of anger. Well and good, Mercald." To him, aloud, she said. "Think, now, if you are disgraced, will you be disgraced alone?"

"It was my fault alone. No other Birder would . . . "

"Tush, boy. I wasn't talking of Brightfeather out there. I was speaking of *her*, Handbright. If you are disgraced, so will she be disgraced. If you are punished, so will she be punished. If you are put to death—as I have no doubt someone will try to do—then do you think they will not try it with her as well?"

His expression took on all the understanding she could have wished, horror and terror mixed. "But she is a messenger of the Boundless. They would not dare so offend the Boundless. . . ." Then he thought of this and his expression changed. She knew then that there was a functioning mind behind all the milky youth of him, for his eyes became suddenly aware and cold. "By the

Boundless, but they would. Those piles of flopper ex-
crement would try it, to discredit our judging of
them. . . ."

Mavin smiled. "Who? Who are they, boy?"

He drew himself up, blazing. "I am not 'boy'. I am a
Birder of the third degree, judge of the people of the
chasm. I will examine mine own conscience, doer-good,
if that is warranted, but I will not submit to disgrace
which uses matters of conscience as a starting point for
revolt. As to who they are, if you know so much, you
know as well as I. The ones from Nextdown. Bridgers,
mostly, though with casteless ones mixed in, and
Porters and people from Bottommost."

"Led by whom?"

"I don't know. Nor why. But led by someone, I have
no doubt."

"As to that, I can enlighten you. Which I will do,
young judge, if you will come with me toward Bridgers
House. Beedie has gone there to arrange a meeting with
the Bridger elders—only those of Topbridge, mind
you."

"It is customary for Bridgers to wait upon the Birder
caste," he replied in a stiff voice, now growing accustomed to his anger and making use of it.

"Come off it, Birder. If the rebels have used Handbright's condition to discredit your caste, it was you
who gave them the opportunity. Take off your robes.
Put on something dark and inconspicuous, and we will
walk outside the light of the lanterns. We are sneaking
away to a secret meeting, not leading a procession of
dignitaries." And she smiled at him, nodding toward
the door to give him leave to go, listening throughout all
this to the voice of Handbright behind her, threading
endless chains of unstrung words with her song.

They left Handbright singing, making no attempt to
guard her, Mavin doing so in the hope the skulkers had
not been directed to start overt trouble so soon, and
Mercald with the conviction that she was safe, would
always be safe in a Birders House. Leaving dignity
behind, they skulked down the twisty ways among the

dwellings and shops, up and down half flights of stairs, out onto Fisher platforms and back again, staying out of the light of the lanterns, away from the alley corner gapers and chatterers. They encountered Beedie only a little way from the Bridgers House.

"Rootweaver says she can meet with us in about an hour, Mavin. Mercald. You look very different without your robes. Was it you got Mavin's sister pregnant?"

He began the stuttering, fluttering, pale then red once more, only to be stopped in midflutter by Mavin's saying, "Of course he did, sausage girl. He's the only one innocent enough to have done it without realizing what a mess it would make. Don't tease him about it. He's troubled enough as is, and will be more when we finally figure out what needs to be done."

Chapter 4

The buildings of Topbridge burgeoned at the edges of the bridge like growing things, room atop room, lump on lump, anchored by fine nets of twig roots to the buildings below, connected across alleys by twisting, tendril-like flights of stairs. Fishers' roosts jutted like rude tongues from this general mass; every roomlet sprouted corbeled parapets; machicolations perforated the edges, allowing a constant shower of debris to float downward. The city was fringed with vertical roots which fell from the great supporting catenaries into the everlasting murk of the far-below, pumping life up into the mainroots and thus into the city. Along some of these verticals, new towers spun themselves in airy insubstantiality, a mere hinted framework of hair roots and a plank or two awaiting the day they would be strong enough to support a floor, a wall, a roof.

Water fell occasionally from the green leafy sky, a kind of sweet rain or sticky dew, and children ran about in it with their mouths open and tongues stuck out, whooping their pleasure at the taste as their elders made faces of annoyance and wiped the dew from their hands with gestures of fastidious displeasure. Everyone wore fishskin hats on days like this, to keep the sticky rain from coating their hair, and all the awnings were put up, adding to the general appearance of haphazard efflorescence.

This clutter of room upon room, tiny balconies jutting over other such balconies, flat roofs forming the front porch of still other dwellings, all the higgledy-piggledy disarrangement of the place gave way here and there to more open spaces, commons where market stalls surged at the foot of the surrounding structures, flapping with woven awnings and banners like a net full of fishes. Wide avenues ran the length of the bridgetown; narrower alleys twisted across it. Carts rumbled up and down, hawkers cried the flavor of tea, the strength of liquor, the fieriness of exotic spices from Midwall—culled from the parasitical vines which grew there and there alone. Harvesters stalked about vending quantities of root nodules from gaping sacks, or wall moss in bulk, as well as vine fruits, thickic herb, dried strips of net-caught flattree leaves and fifty other viands as strange and odd-smelling.

The favorite place for meetings, whether planned or spontaneous, was Midbridge Market, and the most favored of the stalls there was that of Tentibog the Teaman. There were those who said Tentibog traded with the pombis aloft, that nothing else would explain how he obtained herbs unobtainable by other men, at which Tentibog only laughed and talked of the quality of his water, procured at great expense from some distant, secret water-belly. Whatever his secrets, his place was so crowded that it virtually assured anonymity. Anyone might be there, might meet anyone else, might engage in a moment's conversation or a morning's philosophical discussion without anyone else wondering at it or commenting upon it. So it was that Beedie and Mavin encountered Rootweaver there, and the three of them happened upon Mercald the Birder—dressed in simple trousers and shirt and unrecognizable therefore—and the four of them drank Noon Moment tea while deciding the fate of the chasm.

Rootweaver had ordered the third pot by the time Mavin had finished talking, Beedie marveling the while at the things she had said and had not said. "Because we are what we are, my sister and I," Mavin had emphasized, "does not mean we are not what you supposed my sister to be—a messenger of the Boundless. Indeed, by this time, I believe we are both such messengers, sent to help you out of a difficulty."

"Out of mere kindness, I suppose," Rootweaver had said, somewhat cool in manner.

"Oh, I think not. If the Boundless uses us as its messengers, surely it takes into account what will make us act. I am moved out of sympathy for my sister, whom I owe a debt. And out of regard for your people, who until now have treated her kindly."

Rootweaver toyed with her teacup, one of the Potters' best, circled with lines of rippling color and pleasant to the touch. When she spoke at last, it was with some hesitation. She did not wish to offend Mavin, nor the Boundless, if it came to that, but she was acting eldest, and that carried certain imperatives. "Mavin— see, I call you by your name, thus offering a measure of friendship and trust—you ask that we take your . . . sister into Bridgers House. You make a persuasive case that her life is in danger where she is. No! You need not cite further incident. I am inclined to believe you. We are not so blind in Bridgers House we cannot see unrest or hear the result of manufactured demonstrations of discontent.

"So, well and good. But what would occur if this woman were taken into Bridgers House? Those responsible for rumor and riot would soon learn she is gone from Birders. They would seek her out. Our house is full of Maintainers and workmen who come and go. There is no locked room so remote that its existence might not become known if a search were going on. So on the one hand a woman will have disappeared, on the other hand there will be a locked room at Bridgers

House. What will the rumormongers make of that?"

There was a lengthy silence. Beedie sighed, tapping the table with her own teacup. "She's right, Mavin. That wouldn't keep the birdwoman safe."

"Besides which," Rootweaver went on in her calm voice, "you give us no real reason to assist you in this way. We would be more sensible to disinvolve ourselves, to stand remote from this Bander-Birder conflict so that our own position would not be threatened."

"The Banders killed my family," Beedie burst out, in a barely suppressed whisper. "Tried to kill me . . . "

"Where is your proof? What proof do you have, child? A cough heard on the stair from Potter's bridge? A sneering look? Suspicious absences? A bit of harassment by officious Banders? Well, here is a judge. Tell me, Mercald, would you convict the Banders on this evidence?"

Mercald flushed, then turned pale. "I could not," he whispered. "As you know, Bridger."

"You see," said Rootweaver. "If we have no proof, we cannot take action against the Banders. We cannot even be sure to prevent what evil they may attempt in the future. Because we have no proof, we Beeds and Chafers must protect ourselves. We cannot openly ally ourselves with Birders who may fall into disrepute. We cannot have ourselves accused of blasphemy because we offer protection to a person alleged to be a false messenger, perhaps a servant of Demons. . . ."

"I have said Handbright means much to me. I cannot take her away with me until she is delivered of the child she carries. If she remains here, it is at peril to her life. And you say you will not help me?" Mavin spoke in that flat, incurious voice Beedie had heard before, an ominous voice in that it gave nothing away.

"I didn't say that," replied Rootweaver, pouring Mavin more tea. "I merely said that you asked a great deal and offered nothing much in return except information we were already aware of. Now—if you were willing to take on a job of work for us. . . ."

"Ah," said Mavin. "So now we come to it."

"We come to it indeed, if you wish. I have something in mind." Rootweaver leaned forward to speak softly, intently, making closed, imperative gestures with her fingers, hidden from others in the room by their huddled bodies. Mercald and Beedie listened with their mouths open.

Mavin feigned uninterest. When Rootweaver had done, however, she leaned back, stared at the ceiling for a time, then dried her hands on her trousers and held them out. "Done," she said. "Agreed. If you will keep Handbright safe."

"We can only try," the Bridger replied. "We may not succeed once it is known she lodges with us."

Mavin gave her one, brilliant smile. "I think we can improve her chances in that regard. It may not be necessary for anyone to know that the birdwoman is with you at all. And while we are at it, may we test to see if proof of our belief may be found?"

"You may test. You may not foment insurrection merely to see who falls into your mouth." Mercald said this firmly, without doubt, and Beedie gave him a surprised look. For all his milky youth, still he had some iron in him.

"Very well then," agreed Mavin. "Here is what we will do. . . ."

The following day, an hour or so before noonglow, a procession of Bridgers and Birders was seen to enter the marketplace, dressed in the full regalia of office, obviously on some portentous mission. The assembly of so many top caste persons was enough in itself to attract attention, and by the time the call for prayer cried silence upon Topbridge, there were people in every alley and every market stall, on every roof and balcony, waiting to see what would happen.

It was Rootweaver who mounted to the announcement block on the market floor at the very center of the commons, she who cried into the attentive quiet of the place. "People of Topbridge, I speak for the eldest Bridger, Quickaxe, head of chasm council, who is too feeble with age to attend upon you. I am next eldest, next in line to be head of chasm council. I am here to speak about disorder, for disorder has come to the chasm. There has been talk and dissention. A Birder has been assaulted—no, do not draw horrified breath. There is not one of you who did not know of it.

"As you all know, Mercald the Birder received a visitation from a messenger of the Boundless. This is a mystery. We do not understand why the messenger has come. Some, in their foolishness, have accused the Birders of ill doing. Others have gone so far as to question the validity of Birders' judgments, their place to judge at all.

"I come to you all with a message. Tomorrow, during noonglow, the messenger will depart Topbridge. It has come to lead a small group on a quest, toward a greater mystery than any we have spoken of. Mercald, the Birder, will attend upon that quest. Beed's daughter, Bridger, will attend upon it. The Maintainer Roges will attend upon the quest. They go to find the lost bridge. I invite you to witness the going forth.

"There will be no disorder! I serve notice here upon you all. If there is language unfitting the occasion, if there is unruly behavior, if there is childish rebelliousness displayed, those responsible will be brought before swift judgment under chasm rule." Then there was indrawn breath from everyone present. Mavin had been prepared for that, and she heard it with satisfaction. Chasm rule allowed immediate execution of rebels against the order of the bridgetowns by tossing them into the chasm. Privately, she thought it a bit too good for the Banders—at least, those involved in the conspiracy, as she felt most of them probably were. From the corner where she stood, she watched faces, eyes, searching for the quick sideways glance, the covert whisper, the betraying signs of those who had plans that were upset by this announcement. There were many. Too many. Most of them casteless ones, but there were Bridgers among them, and Fishers, and a knot of belligerent-looking Harvesters. She shook her head. Proof! She had all the proof she needed.

Ah, well. Much to do before the morrow. Much explanation, much preparation. Rumor must be spread in the marketplace concerning the treasures of the Lost-bridgers. Beedie must be outfitted for travel, and Mercald, and the 'Tainer Roges. Beedie had not wanted him along, had become rather flushed about it, as a matter of fact, but Rootweaver had insisted. "Where a Bridger goes, a Maintainer goes, Beedie, and that's the rule. In times of danger, a Maintainer is a Bridger's spare eyes, a Bridger's spare nose."

"I can take care of myself," she had replied rebelliously. "I don't need Roges."

"If you will not accept him as a quest mate, then we must send some other Bridger," Rootweaver had replied. "We will not begin a holy quest by breaking the rules. You may be sure someone would notice, and it would throw doubt upon the whole endeavor."

"Rootweaver is right," Mavin had said. "Let be, Beedie. I've met Roges. He's strong, sensible, and seemingly devoted to you, though why he should be, I cannot tell you." At which Beedie had flushed bright red and shut up.

In the night, at the darkest time, a small group of people left Birders House unobserved, carrying something fairly heavy. The placed it in a cart with muffled wheels and took it along the main avenue. The avenue was much darker than usual, for all the lanterns had gone out simultaneously. This happened rarely, but it did happen. If anyone lay wakeful at that time to hear the muffled squeak of a wheel, no one remarked upon it at the time or later. At Bridgers House the cart was unloaded and those who had accompanied it dispersed into the dark. When morning came, there was no evidence of the trip. The cart was back behind Harvesters House from which it had been borrowed. The visiting Harvester, Mavin, who had enquired about the cart, had departed the evening before. There were those in the house sorry to see her go. She had been interested in everything, a good listener to all their tales, all their woes and dissatisfactions, and she had been remarkably

good with the slow-girules, almost as though she under-
stood their strange language. Two of the Harvesters,
meeting over breakfast tea, remarked that it was sad she
would miss the beginning of the quest which was to start
at midday.

"Though she's probably on the stairs to Nextdown by
now, and from there she'll probably see as much as we
will. Likely more. With the crowd there'll be, likely
we'll see nothing or less." Mavin, preparing herself in
the back room at Birders House, would have been
amused.

Time moved toward noonglow. Mercald came out of
the Birders House, together with Brightfeather and half
a dozen others of the Birders, all in their robes and
stoles, tall hats on their heads with feather plumes nodding at the tips. In their midst walked a birdwoman in
her green dress, the silver and blue ribbons flowing as
she walked, calm and easy, humming her song in a quiet
voice.

The woman who had once worn that dress now sat in
a high, comfortable room at Bridgers House, guarded
both day and night. She wore clothes of quite a different
kind. Her hair had been cut and dyed. She did not
resemble the birdwoman at all.

Anyone who went to the Birders House would find it
empty; anyone who looked at the birdwoman in the procession saw that she was lean as a sideroot. There was
murmuring, consternation in some quarters. How could
one accuse the Birders of having interfered with a
messenger of the Boundless when the messenger did not
seem to have been interfered with? Byle Bander, watching from a convenient doorway, slipped inside the house
to report to his dad.

"No sign at all, Dah. None. She was swole like a
water-belly three days ago. I swear. Saw it myself. Not
now, though."

"There's some can use herbs," said the old man in a
dire voice. "We can give it out that they used herbs on
her, made her lose it."

"Ah, but Dah, those herbs come nigh to killing anyone who takes 'em. Everybody knows that. This one is healthy as anything. No sign she was ever sick, and there are those know she was swole three days ago. They're saying it's a miracle already on the street."

The man heaved himself up, face dark with fury. "What are they up to, those Beeds, those Chafers? I ask you. What do they know?"

"Nothing, Dah. How could they?"

"Well it's strange, I tell you. All suddenly now, after doing nothing for days and days, the whole Bridger bunch is talking quest. Talking miracle. Talking to the Birders as though they was cousins. And you noticed how they go around? There's never a time they don't have a Maintainer within reach, knife in his belt, looking, looking. What are they suspecting?"

"Well . . . a lot of 'em have died, Dah. You can't expect they shouldn't notice."

"Accidents," said the old man, sneering. "All accidents. It's that Beed's daughter girl. She's come up from rootburn all full of fury, spreading stories."

"I haven't heard any, Dah. Swear I haven't."

"Well, hear it or not, it's her, I'll tell you. Come up on the roof, boy. We'll see what they're about."

Outside, the procession moved into the commons. The birdwoman moved toward the railing to stand framed by two verticals, posed, all soft as feathers in dress and demeanor, gazing around her with mild eyes. Some of those who had been busy assaulting the Birder only days before had the sense to look ashamed of themselves, and more than one wife whispered angry words to her husband. "You see! You can tell she's holy. You men, putting your filthy mouths on everything wonderful. . . ." "Pregnant, is she? Well, she's about as pregnant as my broom handle, husband. If you'd spend more time making nets and less time in chatter, we'd be better off and the Boundless would be gratified, I'm sure." Mavin, looking at them out of Handbright's face, read their lips, their expressions, and smiled inwardly.

The Birders moved toward her, setting up poles, banners, making a screen around her on all sides except outward toward the chasm. They roofed it with scarves, and Mavin was hidden from their view. The call for prayer sounded, a narrow cry, a climbing sound which rose, rose, upward into the green sky. Floppers honked in the root wall. Birds sang. High above them a breeze shook the leaves of the flattrees and the sweet dew fell. Noonglow came. The Birders drew the screen away.

All the assembled people gasped at the white bird which perched at the edge of the chasm, unbelievably huge and pure, more a symbol than a living thing, hierarchic and marvelous.

Mercald moved forward, a traveler's pack on his back, Beedie coming to stand beside him, then Roges. "Show us the way," Mercald called to the bird in his high, priest's voice. "Show us the way, messenger."

Mavin spread her wings, dived from the edge of the bridge, caught the air beneath her and whirled out into the hot, uprising draft. She circled upward, twice, three times, gaining height with which to circle above the bridge, crying in a trumpet voice as she did so, then outward once more and down, down into the depths and out of sight. Mercald struck the bridge floor with his staff, cried, "We follow, messenger. We follow." The three of them moved resolutely toward the stair to Nextdown as the crowds pushed back in religious awe. A group of ordinary people Messengers assembled at the chasm side, strapping on their flopperskin wings, leaping one by one out into the same warm updraft to circle away up-chasm and down-chasm, carrying word of what had happened.

Behind the questers on the roof of his house, Slysaw Bander pounded the parapet with his fists. "They know something, Byle, I tell you they know something. They've got something in their mouths besides their teeth. Something big. Something wonderful. The lost bridge went down in the long ago, so they say, with treasure on it. Treasure we can't even think of, boy, because we've lost the secrets of it. Can you imagine? Well, I've need of treasure right now. I need to put it in many pockets, boy, and the Banders are running shy of enough of it. So I'm not going to let them get it all by theirselfs. Pack us some gear, boy, and go tell your cousins. There'll be two expeditions going down, one to lead and one to follow—one to find, and one to take it away from them.''

''But, Dah! It makes me fearful to hear you talk so. Fearful to think what they may be up to. There's only a few of the old Beeds and Chafers to have done with and you'll be eldest. Why go away now? We're close, Dah. Real close.''

''Because they're onto something, boy. And whatever it is, we've got to know. The other'll wait. None of 'em'll get younger while we're away. Come on now, hop.'' And Byle Bander hopped, unaware that when the group left the house and headed for the stairs down which Mercald had gone, they were observed with considerable satisfaction by Rootweaver herself.

''You see, cousin,'' she said to the eldest, who sat well wrapped in an invalid chair at the teashop table. ''While it won't do as proof, still it goes far to establish that Mavin was right.''

''But who is she?'' the old man said wonderingly. ''What is she?''

''A wonder, a Demon, a messenger of the Boundless,'' replied Rootweaver. ''Mavin Manyshaped. One who can see farther than we have had to learn to do, cousin.''

''Well then,'' he said, ''what is to happen now?''

''According to Mavin, the announcement of a quest, particularly one rumored to have treasure as a part of it, will draw the villains out where they may be seen and proof assembled against them. Mercald goes with the questers to witness such proof and to remove him as a subject of rumor. Beedie goes because Mavin asked for her, and because the girl has an adventurous spirit. Roges goes where Beedie goes.'' Rootweaver refilled their cups, meditatively, gazing at the stair head, now almost vacant. She remembered her own youth, her own adventurous spirit. For her, too, there had been a certain Maintainer. . . .

"Actually, Eldest, they go to find out what is killing the roots of the bridges. We do not say that, for to say it would mean panic, but that is why they go—that is the bargain we have made with Mavin. 'Find out,' we said, 'and put a stop to it.'

"Privately, I believe Mavin would have gone into the chasm to explore it whether we asked her to do so or not," she said. "She is an adventurer first, and whatever else she may be second. This is in her eyes, in the very smell of her skin. Well, as for us, we will wait and see. Guard the pregnant birdgirl, guard ourselves against assassination, warn our fellows on the other bridges, and wait and see."

The old man shook his head. Despite his fragility, his concern for the people he had so long cared for, he found himself in a curious mood. After thinking about it for a very long time, he decided the feeling was one of envy. Wait and see was not what he really wanted to do, and he thought of Beedie and Roges as he had seen them marching off to the stairs with a longing so sharp that he gasped, and Rootweaver had to put his head between his knees until he recovered.

Chapter 5

There was no one else on the stairs when the small group began the descent. They looked back to see the whole rim of the bridge edged with white disks of faces, mouths open in the middle so that it looked like hundreds of small, pale O's along the railing and at every window. "We are already a legend," said Beedie, not without some satisfaction.

"I pray there will be more to the legend than a last sight of us disappearing into the depths," commented Roges. He was staying politely behind her, and Beedie was surprised to find that the thought of him so close rather pleased her. Well, it was a new thing she was doing, unused to travel as she was. It was always good to have familiar things about, rugs, bits of furniture, ones own 'Tainer. With uncustomary tact, she did not mention this to him, knowing that he would not like being compared to cooking pots and sleeping mats. Then, too, perhaps the comparison was not quite fair. Roges was a good deal more useful than a sleeping mat. She flushed, and began to think of something else.

"Do I understand that the white bird was not actually the . . . the messenger which we had received before?" Roges asked. "Actually, Bridger, Rootweaver told me very little."

"Maintainer, the white bird we are following into the depths is named Mavin. She, whatever she is, is sister to that white bird Mercald had in Birders House—the one all the fuss was about. However, everyone thinks it is the same white bird, so if they are intent on doing it harm, they'll have to follow us into the depths to do it."

"And we are not actually upon a quest to find the lost bridge? I gathered that much."

"Roges," Beedie sighed, calling him by name for the first time in her life without noticing she was doing it, "We're going to find what's eating the roots. Because Rootweaver and all the elders are frightened half out of their wits. And they're afraid to talk about it or go down into the depths themselves for fear it will cause an uproar. So they've maneuvered Mavin into doing it for them. Now that's the whole truth of it."

"Ah," said Roges, turning pale, though Beedie did not see it, for which he was grateful. "There's been talk about something eating the roots. Whispers, mostly. No one seems to know anything about it, except that some of them are dying. Well. How . . . interesting to be going on such a mission."

Then he fell silent and said nothing more for quite some time while he tried to decide how he was going to act now that he knew what the mission was about. Eventually he reached the conclusion that he would still have volunteered to come even if he had known the whole truth; that being part of the group selected for such a mission was gratifying; and that while the journey had suddenly gained certain frightening aspects, he did not regret that aspect of it. Besides, nothing could have kept him from going wherever Beedie went, though he carefully did not explain this to himself. After a little time he felt better about it, and actually smiled as he followed Beedie on down the seemingly endless stair.

"What was it you said about not stopping at Nextdown?'' Mercald asked her. ''I didn't understand that part.''

''Mavin said she would meet us on the stairs before we get to Nextdown, and she doesn't want us to go to Nextdown at all if we can help it. She thinks old Slysaw has been building strength there, and likely we'd be set upon. It's important that they not lay hands upon you.''

''How would they know we are coming? Are the Banders set to assault any Birder who shows up?'' Mercald was edgy with uncertainty, fearful and made touchy by his fear.

''Mavin thought old Slysaw had probably hired a Messenger or two. We know Slysaw is up on Topbridge. One of the Chafers from Bridgers House saw him. So he might have sent word ahead of us to Nextdown. She says she'll be very surprised if he didn't.''

''I didn't know there was a way around Nextdown,'' commented Roges, hearing this for the first time.

''Neither does she. But Mavin says if there is a way, she will have found it by the time we get there. She thinks there may be some construction stairs used by the Bridgers in times past that will duck down this side and join the stairs to Midwall farther on.''

''If so,'' said Mercald, ''I'll wager they've rotted away by now. Nextdown is the second oldest of all the bridges, and it hasn't been renewed at all. Any construction stairs would be lair for crawly-claws by now.''

''I thought Topbridge was the second bridgetown built,'' said Roges. ''Before the fall of Firstbridge.''

Mercald shook his head. ''Nextdown had been started before Firstbridge was destroyed. There were already stairs down to it, which is how a few Firstbridgers escaped. Then, it was from Nextdown they moved up to build Topbridge. It's all in the records we have left at the Birders House. Not that they're complete in any sense. Mostly they're things that were rewritten from memory after Firstbridge was broken.''

''Do they say where we came from, Mercald?'' Beedie had been curious about this ever since Mavin had spoken of the wide world above the chasm.

"Only that we came from somewhere else, long ago. We lived on the surface under the trees until the beasts drove us out. And why that happened is a mystery. Some say it's because we sinned, disobeyed the Boundless. Others say the Demon Daudir brought it upon us out of wickedness."

"I haven't ever heard of the Demon Daudir!" Beedie was indignant. "If it's an old story, why haven't I heard it?"

"Because it's accounted heresy," replied Mercald. He had stopped for a moment at a place the stair root they were on switched to another one, heading back along the root wall. Stairs were made by pulling a sideroot diagonally along the root wall as far as it would go, then cutting steps into it and building rails where necessary. Except for the short stretch between Potter's bridge and Miner's bridge, one root was not sufficient for the whole distance and crossovers were needed. At these crossover points, small platforms gave space to rest. Travelers caught between bridges by nightfall sometimes slept there, too. Mercald stopped to take off his high, feathered hat, folding it up with some care and stowing it away in his pack wrapped in a handkerchief. His robes were next, and when he had finished all the regalia was hidden away and he appeared to be merely another traveler. "Daudir was supposed to be a Demon who arrived out of the Boundless in the time of our many-times-great forefathers. She brought disaster upon our world, so it is said, and our own troubles were the result. However, this is not in accordance with the Birders' teachings, so we don't talk of it."

Beedie wondered if Mavin knew the legend, and if so what she thought of it. "Why isn't it in accordance, Mercald? Is it a story?"

"Everything is a story," muttered Roges, unheard.

"It isn't a story," Mercald said. "But it is doctrine. Do you want to hear it?"

"If it isn't too much trouble."

"As a Birder, I have no choice. Trouble or no, I must tell what is to be told. That's what Birders are for. So.

Let me follow you and Roges, and that way you can hear me as I talk. . . .

"*The Story of the Creation of All.* Ahem. Time was the Boundless lived alone, without edge or limit, lost in contemplation of itself. Time was the Boundless said, 'I will divide me into parts and compare one part against the next to see if I am the same in all parts of me, for if there is difference in anything, in this way may I discover it.'

"So the Boundless divided itself, one part against another part, and examined all the parts to see if difference dwelt among them, and lo, there was difference among the parts for what one part contained was not always what another part contained.

"So the Boundless was long lost in contemplation, until the Boundless said, 'Lo, I will divide me smaller, in order to see where the difference lies.' And the Boundless divided itself smaller yet, finding more difference the smaller it was divided. . . ."

"I don't understand that at all," murmured Beedie to Roges.

"It would be hard to tell the difference between Beedie and Beedie," Roges whispered. "But if you divided yourself in pieces, I suppose it would be easy enough to tell your left foot from your elbow." He smiled behind his hand.

"Until at last," Mercald went on in full flight of quotation, "the Boundless was many, myriad, and the differences were everywhere. Then did the Boundless hear the crying of its parts which were lost in the all and everything. 'Woe,' they cried, 'we are lost'."

"I should think so," muttered Beedie. "What a thing to do to oneself."

"So it was the Boundless created Bounds for its parts and its differences, and places wherein they might exist, that the differences might have familiarities in which to grow toward Boundlessness once more. . . ."

"And a good thing, too," said Beedie. "Now, what has that to do with not believing in Daudir the Demon?"

Mercald shook his head at her, provoked. "Obviously, this chasm is a familiarity, a Bounded place which was created for us by the Boundless. We are the differences who live here. If it was created for us by the Boundless, then it can have nothing to do with Demons or devils or anything of the kind. All of that is mere superstition and beneath our dignity as people of the chasm. Doctrine teaches that all differences are merely that—differences. Not necessarily good or evil." He then fell silent, climbing a little slower so that the other two drew away from him.

"Try not to tread on him," said Roges. "All the really religious Birders are sensitive as mim plants. You touch them crooked, and they curl up and ooze. As judges go, Mercald isn't bad. He's true to the calling."

"You speak as though some might not be," she said, surprised.

"Some are not. I come from Potter's bridge, and we had Birders there as judges I would not have had judge my serving of tea for fear they'd condemn me under chasm rule. It was pay them in advance or suffer the consequences, and those among us too poor to pay suffered indeed."

"Wasn't it reported to the chasm council?"

"Oh, eventually. Before that, however, there was much damage done. In the end, it was only three of them were judged by their fellows and tossed over, two brothers and a sister, all corrupt as old iron." He moved swiftly to one side of the stair, reaching out toward a ropey root that hung an arm's length away. It was dotted with tender nodules, the green-furred ones called root mice, and he cut them cleanly from the root to place them in the pouch at his belt. "Enough for the three of us," he said. "And some left over for breakfast." He knelt, peering through the railings. "Ah. Look there, Bridger. In that little hole in the biggest root along there, see—behind the three little ones in a row."

She knelt beside him, searching until her eyes found the waving claws, moving out, then in, then out once more. "A crawly-claw," she whispered. "Do you suppose we could get him?"

"Do you suppose we should? With a judge following after? We're not Hunter caste." He was laughing at her, she knew, but at the moment she didn't mind.

"I caught one once," she confessed, blushing at the memory of her illicit behavior. "A little one. I had to hunt all up and down the root wall for enough deadroot to cook it, but it was worth it. Isn't it all right if we're out on the root wall?"

"We're not on the root wall. We're on the stairs. And there's likely to be a party coming up or coming down past us any time. No. Likely hunting a crawly-claw would take longer than would be prudent."

"It's true. They pull back in and disappear, and you have to burrow for them. Well, all right," she agreed. "But we'll keep an eye out for any wireworms. And if we see any, we get them, whether there's a Hunter around or not." Beedie had never had enough fried wireworms, and there were never enough in the market to satisfy her appetite, even if she had had enough money to buy them all.

Mercald had caught up with them, evidently restored to good humor by his time alone. He moved ahead of them now, after admiring the crawly-claw and quoting in great detail several recipes for preparation of the beasts, and they continued their downward way. Beedie, her legs accustomed to hard climbs by hours each day spent in spurs, did not feel the climb, but she noticed that both the others stopped from time to time, wriggling their legs and feet to restore feeling numbed by the constant down, down, down.

They had not come far enough yet for the quality of light to change much. It was still that watery green light the Topbridgers knew as daylight, full of swimming shadows cast by the leaves as they moved in winds from outside the chasm. Beedie remembered the light on Nextdown as being less watery and more murky, darker. She had heard that on Midwall and Miner's bridge,

lanterns were used except at midday, and of course on
Bottommost, they were needed at all times. She had
heard, also, that the eyes of the people on Bottommost
were larger, but this might well not be true. Surely
travelers from Bottommost would have come to Topbridge from time to time, but she had never noticed any
strangers with very large eyes.

They went on. A group of chattering Porters passed
them going up, followed not much later by a second
group, their legs hard and bulging with climbing muscle.
A Messenger swooped by on flopperskin wings, calling
to them as they went, "Luck to the quest, Bridger. . . ."
before falling away out of sight in the direction of Potter's bridge. The light began to fail; the stairs became
hard to see. Far below them lights began to flicker in a
long line, stretching from the root wall out across the
chasm in a delicate chain, growing brighter as they
descended. They stopped at the railing to look down,
hearing the voice behind them without surprise, almost
as though they had expected it.

"What took you so long?" asked Mavin. She stood in
the shadow, half-hidden behind a fall of small roots,
almost invisible.

"We had no wings, ma'am," said Roges, grinning at
Mavin with what Beedie considered astonishing familiarity.

"Fair blow, Maintainer. Well, I had hoped to tell you
of a sideway by this time, some kind of trail or climb
around Nextdown. I've looked. Up the wall and down
it, behind the roots and before them. Nothing. What
was there has rotted away and been eaten by the
wireworms long since."

"So we must go to Nextdown after all," said Beedie.

"Where needs must, sausage girl. However, we'll not
do it without a little preparation. There's a house full of
Banders near the stair—the very house your Aunt Six
told me you used to occupy, Beedie. Evidently all the
Bander kin from upstairs and down have come to fill it
full, and every window of it has eyes on this stairway.

They've been warned we're coming. There's talk of assault and the taking of a Birder hostage. So, lest harm fall . . . ''

"Lest harm fall?" questioned Mercald, fearfully.

"We shall commit a surprise. As soon as we figure one out. However, why don't we have something to eat, first. Have you supplies, Maintainer?''

"Fresh root mice, ma'am. And things less fresh brought from Topbridge. We can have a cold supper.''

"No need for that. There's a cave in the wall, just here, behind these roots, and a pile of deadroot in it enough to warm twenty dinners. There is also a convenient air shaft which guarantees we will not suffocate in our own smoke. Even if all this were not so near and so convenient, I would want it to be a good bit darker before we attempt to go past that Bridgers House. So we might as well rest a while and enjoy our food.''

"We saw a crawly-claw, Mavin. I wanted to hunt it, but Roges said the Hunter caste might catch us at it.''

"Are they especially delicious, girl?''

"They are the best thing next to wireworms. Even better, sometimes.''

"Then we'll have to try and hunt one down, somewhere along the way, Hunter caste or no.'' She wormed her way behind the bundle of roots, showing them the way into the cave. The sight of it surprised them all, for it was lit with one of the puffed fish lanterns glowing softly to itself in the black. Snaffled from Nextdown by a strange bird, said Mavin with some amusement. There was also a vast pile of deadroot, looking as though it had fallen there rather than been gathered in. Roges set about building a fire, laying his supplies ready to hand on a spread sheet of flopperskin.

"I didn't know there were caves in the root wall.'' Mercald was indignant, as though the existence of anything he did not know of was an affront to his priestly dignity.

"I think your people have become so caste-ridden, priest, that they do not use their humanish curiosity any longer. You have no explorer caste, do you? No. Nor any geographers? Your adventurous young are not encouraged to burrow about in the root wall?''

"Well, in a manner of speaking," Beedie interrupted. "Bridger youngsters climb about from the time they can walk. I did."

"Always under supervision, I'll warrant. Always learning methods or perfecting skills. Well, it doesn't matter; it's only a matter of interest to me. In looking for a way around Nextdown, you see, I have found a number of curiosities, and I merely wonder that the people of the chasm seem unaware of them. For example, there is another cave somewhat below us which happens to be occupied by a strangeness.''

"Occupied?" Roges looked up from his folding grill, interested. "Someone living in the wall? A Miner, perhaps?''

"A person. He tells me his name is Haile Sefalik; by profession, a theoretician; in actuality a stranger, an outlander, not belonging in this chasm at all. He tells me he has come here for difference, for where he was before was same. I invited him to join us for supper.''

Roges made a face and turned to his pack for another handful of the root mice. He was slicing them into a pan with bits of dried flopper meat and a bulb of thickic. He did not comment. Mavin watched their faces, interested in the ways they received this news: Mercald fearfully; Roges with housekeeperish resignation; Beedie with delight.

"How wonderful! What is he, Mavin? I don't know what a theo—a theor whatever is.''

"I'm not at all certain, sausage girl. That's why I invited him. He looks hungry, for a start, so I presume a theoretician is not anything practical like a Harvester or a Bridger. He is living in an unimproved cave, so I presume it isn't something useful like a Miner or Crafter. There is a sort of dedication in his expression which reminds me of you, Mercald, but he has no regalia at all.''

"What is he doing, then? In his cave?''

"So far as I can tell, he sits and thinks.''

"Only that?" asked Mercald, scandalized.

"Only that. He's being fed by the slow-girules. I saw two of them come in and leave him a few nodules while I was there. They talked at him, and he talked back at them, and they purred." She smiled again, then held up one finger. "Shhh. I think I hear him on the stairs."

There was a slow tread on the stairs, interrupted by frequent stops. Beedie ran to the cave entrance and peered between the roots, seeing a dark shape silhouetted against the lights of Nextdown, below them. "I know why it does that," said a voice in a tone of pleased amazement. "It's obvious."

"You know why what does what?" asked Beedie, coming out onto the stairs. "Why what does what?"

"I know why it feels colder here than it does up above, among the trees. They always say it is because we are closer to the river, here, with more moisture in the air. Nonsense. We've come down a long way. There's more atmosphere, more heat capacity, and the thicker air cools us faster. That's all. I hadn't thought about that until now. Interesting, isn't it." The person turned toward her, not seeing her. "Different. Not the same at all." He moved blindly toward the place in the roots from which she had emerged, feeling his way between them to the firelit space beyond.

"Who's 'they'?" asked Beedie. "I never heard 'they' say that, about the river and the moisture."

"They," said the man, moving steadily toward the fire and food. "You know. Them."

Beedie had no idea about them. She shook her head and followed him, seeing Mavin grasp him by one arm and lead him to a convenient sitting stone. He was dressed all in ragged bits and pieces, and his face was one of mild interest, unfocused, as though he did not really see any of them even while he took food from Roges' hands. He had shaggy, light hair and a wild-looking moustache and beard which drooped below his chin, wagging gently when he spoke. The color of his eyes was indeterminable, somewhere between vacant and shadow. After a long pause during which no one said anything, he murmured, "Perhaps it was some other place they said it about. That it was colder lower down. Because it was wetter. Perhaps that was it."

"What other place was that?" Mercald asked, suspiciously. "Nextdown? Midwall?"

The man chewed, swallowed, spooned another mouthful up before considering this question. "Oh, not any place very local, I'm afraid. Elsewhere, I think. Before I came here at all."

"You came from elsewhere," commented Mavin. "Perhaps from the place the ancestors of these chasm dwellers came from? Or from the southern continent?"

"Elsewhere," he replied, gesturing vaguely at the rock around them, as though he had permeated it recently. "It started with liquids, you know. *They* didn't understand liquids. Local geometry is non-space-filling. Icosohedra. Triginal bipyramids. Oh, this shape and that shape, lots of them. More than the thirty-two that fill ordinary space, let me tell you. That's why things are liquid, trying to pack themselves in flat space, and that's what I told *them*.

"*They* couldn't deal with it. *They* wanted order, predictability, regularity. Silly. Local geometry can be packed, I said, just not in flat space. So, I said, give them a space of constant curvature and they'll pack. All *they* did was laugh. I took some liquids to a space of constant negative curvature to show *them* it would crystallize, and it sucked me up. One minute, there. Poof. Next minute, somewhere else. Somewhere different, thank the Boundless. Boundless. That's a local word for it. Picked it up from someone on the stairs out there. *Boundless*. Good name for it."

"I'm sure the Boundless would be gratified at your approval," said Mercald, much offended.

"Shhh," calmed Mavin. "The man's a guest in our midst."

"*They* said every place was like the place I was. Infinite replications of sameness. They called it translational symmetry. Well, I determined to find difference no matter what it took. So I left there and came here.

It's different here. It's local. Poof and feh on translational symmetry."

"I thought you said you got here by accident," said
Beedie, trying to make sense out of the person. "By
some curvature or other."

"Yes. Both. Hardly anything is mutually exclusive
when you really think about it. You can't look at things
too closely. The more precisely you look at one thing,
the more uncertain the others get. If we locate me
precisely here, how I got here becomes increasingly
unsure. Tell you the truth, I don't remember."

"Reality has many natures," said Mercald in his most
sententious voice.

"That's the truth," said the theoretician, focusing on
the priest for a moment before drifting away again.
"That's the truth, so far as it goes, at least." He chewed
quietly to himself, smiling at his own thoughts. "Surfaces," he murmured. "Edges. Reality has edges."

"That's the truth," Beedie muttered to herself. "So
far as it goes." She glared at Mavin. "What did we need
him for?"

"Need? Well, sausage girl, what do we need you for?
To make life more interesting. He's different, isn't he?"

Mercald circled the theoretician in slow, ruminative
steps, eating, staring, eating. At last he said, "What do
you mean, reality has edges?" Receiving no response,
he repeated the question, finally driving it through with
a kick at the stone the man was sitting on. "Edges?"

The theoretician put his plate down, picked up a
length of root from the floor of the cave. "You see this?
This is a system. It has surfaces. It has extent. It has size
and corners and edges and impurities and irregular-
ities." He put it down, searched for a stone, found one.
"This one, too. Here's another. Not the same, not the
same at all. And another one yet. All local. Everything's
local. Local."

The other three looked at one another; Mercald kept
on with his circling; at last it was Roges who said,
"So?"

"Not to *them!* Oh, no, not to *them.* To them, every-thing is the same. In all directions. Forever. No edges. No corners. *They* used to scream at me. 'What do you do about surface states?' As though that meant some-thing. I thank the Boundless for surface states. Show me something, anything without surface states! Anything at all! There's nothing like that in reality. But they didn't understand. Just went on inventing 'ons. Polarons. Plasmons. Phonons. Exitons. Vomitons and shitons soon to come. Feh.''

Beedie murmured, "I don't know, Mavin. It seems to me we ought to let him go back to his cave and start worrying about the Banders."

"Banders," screamed the theoretician in a sudden ex-pression of fury. "Infinite lattices. Homogeneous deformation. Idiots."

"I really think it's something religious," said Mercald to Mavin in a thoughtful voice. "There's a fine kind of frenzy about it. Of course, it might be heretical, but it sounds quite like doctrine." He regarded the theoreti-cian almost with fondness.

"We'll take him with us," said Mavin. "If he wants to go. Thinker, do you want to come with us?"

The man shook his head, then nodded it, reaching into the general pan for the last of the fried root mice. "If it will be different where you are going. I've mod-eled this place. There's nothing left to do here."

"He means he has realized it," said Mercald with satisfaction. "I'm beginning to understand him. It is definitely religious, after all." He stroked the theoreti-cian's shoulder, wrinkling his nose at the feel of the rags. "I've got an extra shirt I can lend him."

"Ah," said Mavin. "I'm glad you find him sympa-thetic, Mercald. I wonder if he has any practical use at all." She stretched herself on the cave floor, seeming, to Beedie's eyes, to flow a little, as though she shaped her-self to the declivities of the place. "Thinker, will you solve a problem for me? Give me an answer?"

"Answers? Of course. I always know the answer.

After I see the problem, of course. Not before. They're always terribly simple, answers. Which one do you need?''

''We need to get to the stairs below Nextdown—that's the bridge just below us—without being seen by anyone on Nextdown. There is no other stair and no root climbable by any of us but perhaps Beedie here.''

''Ah,'' said the theoretician. ''Might one ask why?''

''There are a dozen large men at the end of this stair who are determined to do us harm,'' said Mavin, without changing expression. ''Is that reason enough?'' She had been watching Beedie's bright, excited face and was determined not to change into some huge climbing shape which would solve all problems and take all the fun out of the expedition. Besides, Shifting was too easy. Sometimes it was more fun to plot one's way out of trouble. This praiseworthy thought was interrupted.

''Shhh,'' said Roges, moving to throw his jacket over the fish lantern. ''I hear voices. Someone coming down.'' They fell silent, listening, hidden as they were in the dark of the cave, the last glowing coals of the fire hidden from the entrance by their bodies. There was the sound of a dozen pairs of feet, a malignant mutter, a phlegmy cough.

''I smell smoke,'' said someone from outside. Byle Bander's voice. ''Smoke, Dah.''

''Well of course you smell smoke, idiot boy. There's Nextdown no more than a few hundred steps down. This time of evening when don't you smell smoke? Everybody's cooking their dinner, and good time to do it, too. I'm hungry enough to eat for six.''

''You think the Birder's gone on down? You think our fambly took 'em, at Nextdown, Dah?''

''I think that's probable, boy. In which case, we'll have a high old time finding out from that Birder what they're going after.''

''And Beedie. I get to ask Beedie, Dah. That and a few games, huh? She's one I've been wanting to play a few games with for a long time. . . .'' The voices faded away into silence, footsteps echoing up the stair for a time, then nothing.

"Ah," whispered Mavin. "So we are not only expected below, but followed after as well."

"They won't find us down there," said Beedie. "But they'll know we have to be somewhere."

"It's all right, sausage girl. They won't come searching back up the stairs until morning. Well, Birder. Was their conversation proof enough for you?"

Mercald gestured impotently. "What did they say? They would ask me questions. They would play games with Beedie. Can I prove dishonorable intent?"

"Rootsap," said the theoretician. "I've been thinking about rootsap. The way down, you know. Rootsap."

"Poisonous," said Beedie. "Eats through your skin."

"Not at the temperature of the chasm at this altitude at this time before midnight," said the theoretician. "Which is the coolest time of the daily cycle in the chasm. A phenomenon which awaits explanation but is undoubtedly the result of a warming and cooling cycle on the surface." He stood up and patted himself, as though taking inventory, though he carried nothing at all. "Knife," he said. "Or hatchet. We need several good sized blobs."

"Knife is quieter," commented Mavin.

Beedie nodded. Mavin took a knife from her hip and went out of the cave, Mercald following her silently. The theoretician merely sat by the coals, his eyes unfocused, staring at the stone around them, muttering from time to time. "Suitable viscosity. Alpha helix. Temperature dependent polymerization. Glop. All local."

Beedie dumped her pouch on the ground and repacked it, taking a moment to put her hair in order, coiling the dark wealth of it neatly into a bun when she had finished. She caught Roges looking at her, and he flushed. "You have lovely hair," he whispered. "I've wanted to say that, you know.''

"That . . . that kind of talk isn't customary, Maintainer," she said stiffly. Then, seeing the pain in his
face, "Roges. You embarrass me. I'm sorry. Nobody
ever said I had nice hair. Aunt Six always says I'm a
scatter-nonny."

"You're not a scatter-nonny," he said. "Don't be
embarrassed. It's just . . . just, I've never had anyone
trying to do me harm before. If anything happens, I
wanted . . . I wanted to have said . . . ''

"I don't think they're going to do you harm, Roges. I
think it's me they're after. And Mercald, maybe. They
don't even know Mavin is here."

His face darkened in a kind of remote anger. "Harm
to you, Beedie, is harm to me. Maintainers are not mere
servants. We are a good deal more than that."

"Polymer," said the theoretician, loudly. "About
now."

Mavin reentered the cave, carrying a huge milky blob
of rootsap on a piece of bark, Mercald just behind her
similarly burdened. They put the blobs down where the
theoretician could see them. "Well, Thinker?"

"Cooler," he directed. "Wherever it's cooler."

Beedie rose, moved around the cave. "It's coolest just
at the entrance, Mavin. There's a draft there."

They put the rootsap down and waited as the theoretician wandered about, examining roots that came
through the cave top, smiling at rocks. At last he came
to the cave entrance and peered at the blobs. "There,"
he said with considerable satisfaction. "You can see the
polymerization beginning." They looked at the whitish
blobs which were turning transparent. "Cut it," he suggested in his mild voice. "Into four pieces. No. Five. I'll
go with you."

Mavin shrugged, took her knife and cut the blobs into
five parts. They resisted cutting, piling up around the
blade. She pushed the blobs apart, for they seemed to
want to rejoin.

"That's funny," said Beedie. "I've never seen it
behave that way before."

"Nighttime," said the Thinker. "You'd have to have seen it at nighttime, when it's cool."

"You've seen it at nighttime before?"

"Well, no. But I thought about it."

"Now what?" asked Mavin. "We've got five blobs, rapidly turning transparent. What now?"

"When they are totally clear, you'll need to pull it through a hole of some kind. Lacking any method of precise measurement, I would say something roughly finger size. Small finger size." He watched with interest as Mavin carried the blobs and the fish lanterns out into the dark. There she found a chunk of tough rootbark and drilled a hole in it with her knife.

"So?" she asked. "Why don't you do one."

"Madam, I am not an experimentalist!" The theoretician turned his back on her, as offended as Mercald had been earlier.

Mavin snorted. "Well, if you won't soil your hands, you won't. Have you any suggestion what I should do next?"

He turned, very dignified in his rags. "You'll need to push the blob through the hole. You'll need to fasten that chunk to something that will hold your weight."

She found a convenient fork in a root and wedged the chunk behind it after pushing some of the blob through the hole with a stick of deadroot.

"That should do," said the theoretician, taking a firm hold on the part of the blob which protruded from the hole and leaning outward into space. "Be sure to make all the holes in the bark just that size. The yield at that diameter will be approximately one hundred man heights. . . ." The blob stretched. He grasped it firmly. It stretched further. He stepped into air, and the blob stretched, becoming a thick rope, a line, a line that went on stretching, bobbing him gently at the end of it like a child's balloon as he sank down below the light of the lantern into darkness. "I thought it would do that," his voice came plaintively up. "I could theorize, but does anyone know what's down below?"

"For all our sakes, I hope it's the stair to Potter's

bridge," muttered Mavin, leaning out into the chasm. "Well, let's make another chunk with a hole in it, sausage girl. However, let me try it first. What works for our strange guest might not work for us. He's fond of saying everything is local."

After another session with knife and bark chunk, Mavin stepped into the chasm and dwindled away at the end of the stretching line, bobbing as she went. The sapline made a thin humming noise as it stretched, a kind of whirring. After a time, when the blob had shrunk almost to nothing, the whirring stopped, and Beedie heard a muffled call from below.

"I guess we try it," she said to Roges, wiping her hands up and down her trousers.

Mercald was dithering at the edge of the drop, peering down, taking a grip, then giving it up, peering down once more. "I . . . I . . . can't . . . let . . . I can't . . ."

"Oh, foof," she spat. "He's got the down-dizzies. I might have known. Mercald. Don't look. I'm pushing some of it through, now take firm hold of it. *Wipe* your hands, ninny. They're all slippery and wet. Here. I'll use my belt to fasten you to it so you can't drop. Now. Roges and I are going to hold you by the hands. Shut your eyes. Now! I mean it. Do what I say, or I'll call the Banders and let them have you. We're holding you. Now. I'm going to let go. You're going down. Just keep your eyes shut. Shut!"

She checked the straps of her pack, wiped her hands once more. "Are you ready, Roges? Roges?"

"Hnnn," he whined through his teeth. "As ready as I'm likely to be, Bridger. I, too, suffer from the down-dizzies, but I suppose it's time to get over it."

She surprised herself, and him, by touching his face, stroking it. "Honestly, Roges. You can get over it. It just takes getting used to. Do what I told Mercald. Just don't look down." She watched as he eased himself over the edge, teeth gritted tight, sweat standing out on his face. He began to drop, and she took firm hold of her own blob, jumping outward with a strong thrust of her legs, stretching it abruptly, so that it twanged, bobbing her up and down in midair. She clung for dear life, cursing her own stupidity.

When she stopped bobbing, she was beside him, falling down the side of the wall in a dream drop, the hairs of the roots tickling her face, occasional small creatures fleeing with squeaks of alarm. She could see only the light of the fish lantern above them, fading into distance, and the lights of Nextdown which came nearer and nearer on her left, until she and Roges were bathed in their glow. He still gritted his teeth, but his eyes were open, darting this way and that, and she knew that he searched for danger to her even as he fought fear for himself.

Then the lights of Nextdown were above them, becoming only a glow against the root wall as the bulk of the bridgetown eclipsed the lanterns. From below she could hear the voice of the Thinker raised in complaint. "*They* would never have thought of that. *Their* systems have no surfaces, and it's totally dependent upon surface. . . ."

"I think I'm going to get very tired of that voice," she said to Roges plaintively.

"I'm tired of it already," he agreed. "Still, we're past Nextdown. We didn't get captured or tortured or held for ransom. We're all alive. And I'm confident we'll find out what's eating the roots, and then we can go home."

Beedie was silent, watching the glow of Nextdown fade above her. "I'm not sure I want to think about . . . home, Roges. Not just yet. I know you get the down-dizzies, but . . . isn't it exciting? Aren't you enjoying it at all?"

There was no time for him to answer. Mavin's voice came out of the blackness nearby. "The stairs are to your right, sausage girl. I'll toss you a line." Then they were drawn down onto the stairs, and she forgot she had asked the question.

Chapter 6

"Where are we?" asked Mercald, his voice still trembling.

"On the stairs to Potter's bridge. Which is not where we particularly want to be," said Mavin. "Nextdown is slightly above us on one hand, Potter's bridge a long way below us on the other hand. Midwall, which is where I need to go in order to reach Bottommost, eventually, is beyond Nextdown, quite the other direction."

"We can work our way along the root wall under Nextdown," said Beedie, not looking at all sanguine about it. "That will bring us to the Midwall stairs."

"I think not," said Mavin. "At least two of us, possibly three, would find such a traverse difficult. I'd rather find another way, if possible."

"Is the idea to escape from those who followed? Who may follow?" The theoretician seemed only mildly interested in the answer to this question.

"No," said Mercald firmly, surprising them all. "The idea is to stay out of reach, but not out of touch. We need proof they are murderers, and for that we must re-

98

main within distance to see and hear what they do, but I'd just as soon not fall into their hands.''

"Hurrah," said Mavin, laughing a little. "Mercald, you put it cogently. We don't want to lose them, Thinker. Only avoid them. Which means I must go up yonder and leave a few clues or whisper a few rumors indicating we've passed them by, don't you think? I suggest the rest of you curl up on the steps—they're rather wide along here—and sleep if you can. I'll return before light.''

"Couldn't we go all the way to the Bottom on the rootsap?" Beedie had enjoyed the drop, once she had quit bouncing. Even that had been interesting. Now she saw with disappointment that the Thinker was shaking his head.

"Limits," he sighed. "Surface to volume, temperature changes, weight a factor, of course. We came about as far as one blob will allow. And now it's too warm.''

Beedie hadn't noticed, but the midnight cool had passed. The winds which swept down the chasm each day from midafternoon to midnight had stopped, and now the warm mists were rising once more. "What would happen if you tried that in the day time?" she asked.

"Plop," said the Thinker, making a vividly explanatory gesture. "Plop. Nothing much left of you, I should think.''

Mavin had already gone. They settled themselves upon the step, backs against the stair risers. Knowing Mercald's fear of heights, Beedie planted pitons and belted him to them. Knowing Roges' pride, she did not do the same for him. Instead, she placed herself between him and the edge, as though unintentionally, a little dismayed at his quiet, "Thank you, Bridger." They settled, not believing they would sleep, but falling asleep almost at once out of sheer weariness.

In remembering it afterward, Beedie was never sure quite what had wakened her. Was it a scratching sound from the stair root itself? Something moving in the root wall? A slight shaking of the stair they rested upon? As though tugged by something pulling at it from below? At first she thought it a dream and merely dozed in it, without concern, waiting to see what odd thing would happen next. Then her eyes snapped wide against the glow of Nextdown, and she felt Roges stiffen behind her, his foot kicking at her involuntarily as he woke.

"What is it?" he hissed.

"Mnn, um," said Mercald. "Wassn. Morning?"

"Unlikely to be volcanic or tectonic," said the Thinker calmly. "Biologic in origin, I shouldn't wonder. Probably zoologic, though there's too little evidence to be sure."

The mists were rising around them, bringing the odors of Bottom, a rich, filthy smell, of rotted things, a soupy odor of growth. Suddenly a miasma struck them, a stench, foul as decaying flesh, sweetly horrible, and they all gagged and gasped in the moment before a rising draft of air wafted it away. The root trembled again, purposefully.

"Something climbing on it, I should say," said the theoretician. "I can compute the probable bulk, knowing the modulus of the root stair we are on, and the degree of movement . . . say something on the order of a thousand two hundred man weights, give or take a hundred."

"How big would that be?" gasped Beedie as another wave of the stink flowed over them.

"Oh, something roughly six or seven men long and a man height and a half through."

Seeing her look of incomprehension, Roges said, "Put another way, something about as long as a four-story building is tall, and as thick through as the Bridgers House living room." The root shook beneath them, a steady, gnawing quiver accompanied by aching vibrations of sound.

The noise covered the sound of Mavin's return, but they heard her voice as she said, "Gamelords! How long has this been going on?"

"Just started," said Roges through his teeth. The smell had grown worse in the last few moments.

"Stay here," she hissed at them in a voice of command. "Don't move. I'll be back in a moment." They had not seen her leave, or return, or leave again, but Beedie's mind flashed quick images of the white bird, and she thought she could hear the whip of air through feathers. They clung to the stair, waiting. It was not long before Mavin returned, calling urgently, "Up. We've got to get off the stair. Either back into the root wall or up onto Nextdown, one or the other. There's a something eating the stairs, something too big to fight." They heard a frantic fluttering among the roots along the wall, exclamations, expressions of fury, a quick hammering, water falling. "Beedie, light a bit of dead-root and get over here."

Roges had it ready, even as Beedie wondered why they had forgotten the fish lantern. Sparks flew, went out, flew again, as Roges cursed at them. Then they caught and the deadroot flared up, centering them in a weird, shadowy dance of light. They saw Mavin along the root wall, perched on a water-belly, a round hole carved into it and another at its bottom draining the water away.

"Tie something to Mercald and I'll haul him over. Roges, help the Thinker. Beedie, put your spurs on."

"I already have them on," she said. "I put them on when the shaking started." She tied Mercald to her with a safety belt and thrust him along a side root, hissing at him. "Close your eyes and crawl, Birder. Crawl, and don't look at anything. Pretend you are crawling under Birders House to check for wall rot. It is very quiet and unexciting, and you'll get to Mavin in just one moment. There." She turned to find Roges at her heels, teeth clenched, eyes fixed ahead. Behind him the Thinker walked along the root, examining the bark as though he had been a Bridger since birth.

"Do you know, the formation of water-bellies occurs at precise intervals dependent upon the diameter of the root involved. I've been thinking . . ."

"Later," snarled Mavin. "Get in here with the rest of us and think about it silently." They slithered together into the water-belly just as the last of its contents drained away, piled untidily in the spherical space, still wet, feeling the tickly brush of little capillary hairs as they huddled, each trying to see out. Mavin had gone out as they came in, and she was perched well above them now, holding the burning deadroot to cast a light upon the quivering stair. The light blinded them; they could not see what shape she had, and only Beedie knew enough about Mavin to wonder. The thought distracted her, and she did not see what the others did until their indrawn breath drew her attention.

It was vast and gray, covered with scabby plaques of hardened ichor or flaking skin, oozing between the plaques thin dribbles of greenish goo which stank. It had an upper end, but no head that they could see. Still, from beneath the upper end came the sound of chewing, gnawing, the rasp, rasp, rasp of hardness biting into the stair root. The thing moved up, up, not seeing them, not looking for them, merely chewing blindly as it came. Then the chewing stopped. The thing quivered obscenely. Its top end began to rise up, sway, a horrible tower of jiggling jelly ending in a circular mouth which sucked, chewed, sucked—and somehow sensed them. The terrible head moved in their direction, cantilevered out from the root stair toward the water-belly, toward the place they crouched, staring, unable to breathe.

Then something flew at the creature's head, something bearing flame, beating at it, burning it. The monster screamed a hissing agonized sigh like a kettle boiling dry. It lashed itself upward, striking blindly, without a target. The torch darted upward, back, down once more, striking at the mouth, again and again. With a last, horrible scream, the mass began to withdraw down the stair, faster than it had come, folding in upon itself, sliding on its own slimy juices, a trail it had laid as it climbed up, going now away and down and out of sight.

Beedie shuddered and then embarrassed herself by beginning to cry. Roges held her tightly, and she could not tell if the wetness on his face was from her or from them both. Mercald was beneath them, his face hidden at the bottom of the water-belly, half suffocated, and she could not imagine how he had come there. The Thinker had withdrawn a pad from among his rags and was making notes, murmuring to himself as he did so.

"Lignivorous. Purulent dermatitis. Unlikely to be a survival trait, therefore pathological. Recently invaded areas would indicate a newly arrived natural enemy perhaps? Or, possibly, use of a toxic substance . . ."

"What do I understand you to say, Thinker?" demanded Mavin, arriving at the opening in the water-belly, panting, holding the torch high so that she could see them. She wore her own shape, or the one Beedie thought of as hers.

"The thing is sick," said the Thinker, putting his pad away. "If not dying, at least not at all well. That skin condition is not normal to the species. So much is evident."

"It wasn't evident to me," muttered Beedie with some hostility. "Does he know everything?"

"Within certain limits, yes," replied the Thinker. "Your attitude of irrelevant hostility is one I have encountered before." He sniffed.

"It's not sick enough that it wouldn't have eaten us, is it?"

The theoretician cocked his head, ruminated over this for a little time, then pronounced: "No. It was eating voraciously. I imagine it will eat almost anything it can get at, though my guess would be it prefers flesh, moist roots and whatever small creatures live upon them."

"There are places not far from where I grew up where they domesticate things like that," said Mavin, thoughtfully. "Not exactly like that, of course. Not so big. Rock eaters. There are said to be smaller ones that eat plants further north. I've never seen them. . . ."

"Quite possibly the same genus," said the Thinker.

"What did you think made the thing sick?"

"A natural enemy, or some accidental ingestion of a naturally toxic substance, or some purposeful contamination by a toxic substance. In other words, something is eating it, it ate something which disagreed with it, or someone is trying very hard to kill it."

"Whoever it is, I'm for them," said Beedie. "I don't blame them a bit."

"Whoever?" asked Mercald, slightly dazed. He had burrowed his way up from the bottom of the water-belly and was now one of them once more, though slightly slimy in aspect. "We would have heard! Where? Even on Bottommost, we would have heard! If anyone had seen one of these things, we would have been notified!"

"Something was destroying the roots, the verticals, Mercald. Rootweaver told us. It's just—no one supposed anything like this." Beedie fell silent, suddenly aware of the implications. "You mean . . . someone is trying to kill those things . . . besides the people on the bridgetowns? Thinker? You mean someone else?"

"My dear person, I have no idea. The who is unimportant. I merely recited the possibilities. If you want me to extrapolate probabilities, it will take me a few moments."

"I don't think we need to belabor our ignorance," Mavin said, heaving Beedie out of the water-belly. "One reason that we came upon this journey was to find this thing—these things. So. We've found it. One. Perhaps there are more. But to find the cause of peril was not the main reason for coming; the main reason is to put an end to that peril, and we are a very long way from knowing how to do that. That we are not alone in the attempt changes nothing, really.

"A thing I do know, however, is that the creature didn't climb all the way up here in one night. That means it didn't go all the way back down, either. I think I saw it ooze itself into a hole some distance below. It's probably been working its way up, night after night, for a long time. It's likely no other of them, if there are more of them, has worked up this high until now, which would explain why they have not been seen or smelled before."

"But now that we have seen, we must send word," said Roges. "The Bridgers must be told."

"Yes, we must send word," agreed Mavin. "We can leave a note nailed to the stair. The first group up from Potter's bridge this morning will find it—and word will be sent. The chewed stairs alone would probably be enough, but we'll describe the creature for them."

"Tell them it fears fire," said Roges. "They'll need to know that." He fell silent, thinking in horror of a bridgetown invaded by such a monster, or monsters, the crushing of little houses, the shrieking of children, the steady rasp, rasp, rasp of its teeth, the stink.

"Light," said the theoretician. "The thing avoids light. It shrank not only from the heat of the torch, but also from the light of it. At least, so I think."

"We will say fire, certainly, and light, possibly," agreed Mavin. "Now. It is written. Do you have a spare piton, Beedie? So. Nailed fast. No one could possibly miss it. I see light above, green light through the leaves. It's time for us to move on before the Banders arrive. Like it or not, we're going to cross the root wall."

"Madam," said the Thinker, "Is it your desire to reach Bottommost?" At her nod he continued, "Bottommost is almost exactly beneath us now."

"Down," said Beedie indignantly. "Three days climb down. Past that thing. Maybe dozens of them. And I'm the only one of us with spurs."

"Down," agreed the Thinker. "With warm updrafts and otherwise calm air, and Bottommost precisely below. I suggest we float."

The others in the group turned to Mavin, exasperated, annoyed, yet despite their annoyance sure that the weird creature had thought of something. "Mavin . . ." Beedie pleaded. "I don't know how to talk to theo—theor-whats-its. Will you talk to him? He makes me tired."

Mavin sighed. "Well, Thinker. Explain yourself. In short and sensible words."

"Well, in layman's terms, there are flattree leaves lying in the Nextdown nets, which are slightly above us. Climbable, I should think. By the young woman with spurs. Or even reachable from the stairs, for that matter. There are half a dozen of them there, at least, very large, tissuey things, soft, pliable, almost like fabric. It has occurred to me that they might be used to manufacture a kind of hyperbolic air compression device . . . let me see, 'wind catchers'. Then, we leap off, one by one, and after an interesting float, we arrive at Bottommost.''

"Splashed into a puddle on the commons, no doubt," said Beedie. "Going about a million man heights every heart beat."

"Dropping at about one man height per heart beat," said the Thinker, annoyed. "Please do not dispute scientific fact with me. It is annoying enough when qualified people do it."

"Would it work?" Beedie pleaded to Mavin. "We could always work along the root wall to the stairs to Midwall. If we take it carefully . . ."

"If we take it carefully, it would take us five days," sighed Mavin, muttering almost inaudibly. She knew that she could solve the problem in a number of ways, all of which required that she gain bulk and shift into something large, crawly or winged, which would involve her in endless explanations. She preferred to remain only a messenger from the Boundless, bird or woman, nothing more than that. It would be safer for Handbright if her sister was not thought to be a devil of some kind even by this friendly group. "Look, I'll test the Thinker's idea. I can always become a bird, so there's no danger. If it works for me, then the rest of you can try it."

"Become a bird?" asked the theoretician. "Is that metaphorical?"

"Never mind," said Beedie, irritated. "Just explain to Mavin what this 'wind catcher' thing is!"

By the time she had climbed to the net, folded and extricated five of the flattree leaves and returned them to the stair, light was shining clearly through the flattrees high above. Rigging the wind catchers seemed to take forever, and Beedie kept reminding herself how long a traverse of the root wall would have taken. Mavin had more or less figured out what the Thinker had in mind and had drawn a little diagram of the way the cords should be strung, from the edges of the leaves to a central girdle. When the first one was done, Mavin fastened the cord girdle around herself then spread the folded leaf along the railing as she climbed over.

"This should be very interesting. It would probably help to jump out as far as possible." The Thinker had observed all this rigging with great interest but without offering to help. "It should unfold nicely, if it doesn't catch on the railing."

"If it doesn't tear, if the ropes hold, if the leaf doesn't rip in the air, if Bottommost is really straight down," muttered Beedie. "Mavin, are you sure you want to do this?"

"It's all right, sausage girl. Besides, I think you can rely on the white bird to help out if anything goes wrong. Now, if it works well for me, rig the others in the same way. You come last. That way you can help the rest of them." And with that she leaped out into the chasm, the faded green of the flattree leaf trailing away behind her. The leaf was small as flattree leaves went, only large enough to carpet a large room, and it caught the air, cupped it, turned into a gently rounded dome that seemed to hang almost motionless in the air as it dwindled slowly, slowly downward.

"Lovely," came Mavin's voice. "Toss Mercald over."

They had already decided that Mercald would have to be tossed. He had turned up his eyes and gone limp at the thought of being dropped into the chasm and was now completely immobile. It was Roges who heaved him over, out into the chasm like a lumpy spear, and they all held their breaths until the leaf opened above him.

"I thought that would work," said the Thinker, tying himself to the girdle. He waited with no evidence of impatience while Mavin spread the leaf behind him, then stepped far into the chasm.

"All right, Roges," she said, knowing without looking that he was sweating again. "Don't look down."

"Beedie." He reached out to touch her shoulder. "You're very pretty, did you know that? Ever since you were little, when you first came to Bridgers House on Topbridge. Even then, you were pretty."

She stared at him, disconcerted again. "I always had skinned knees," she said. "And Aunt Six said my face was never clean from the time I was born."

"Maybe," he replied, trying to smile. "But pretty in spite of it."

"Is this like the hair business?" she asked, growing angry. "You think you're going to get badly hurt or die, so you want to tell me now? Well let me tell you, Roges, I don't go throwing my friends over railings if I think they're going to die. Mavin says she'll catch any of us who have trouble, so if there is trouble just yell and keep yelling. Get up there over that railing and let me spread this thing out." She pushed at him, getting behind him so that he couldn't see the tears on her face. All she seemed to do lately was cry! When he was poised to go, however, shaking so uncontrollably that she could not fail to see it, she could not let him go without a word.

"Roges. When we're down. When we're finished with all this. When we've got the proof that the Banders are murderers and Mavin figures out how to kill those things, tell me then that I'm pretty, will you?" And she pushed him. He fell silently, without a sound, and she found her nails cutting small, bloody holes in her palms until the leaf billowed behind him, cupping air, and he floated after the others.

She spread her own leaf carefully, being sure it would not snag on the railing, then leaped outward—into terror. Her heart thrust upward into her mouth, clogging her breathing. She gasped, sickened, eyes wide with fear, horrified at the weightless, plunging feel of falling, she who had never been afraid of heights before. "You never fell before,'' she screamed at herself. "Oh, I'm going to die. . . ."

Then the leaf opened above her. Warm air rose around her, and the root wall drifted past.

Silence. It was the first thing she noticed. Stairs drummed and clamored beneath feet. Bridgetowns were full of chatter and whine. On the root there was always the noise of the spurs digging in, the chafe of the straps, the blows of hammers or hatchets. But here, here was silence, only the drum of one's blood in one's ears, only the far, falling cry of a bird. Below her, slightly to one side, she could see a movement in the root wall as small creatures burrowed there, then a bare spot where a strange rock . . . a scabrous, oozing rock—the *creature*. There it was, piled into a cave in the wall, only part of its horrid hide exposed. It heaved, breathed, lived, and she dropped below it. The peace of the drop had been destroyed and her stomach heaved in sick revulsion.

She heard Roges calling, twisted herself around to find him. The mound of his leaf was below her, and she called down to him. "Just above you, Roges. Can you see Mercald?''

"Under . . . me . . ." came the call. "Hear . . . town . . ."

She listened, hearing it at last, the far, rattling clamor of a town. What was the word Mavin used? *"Game-lords!"* More and more lately it seemed like a game, some strange, silly game in which no one knew the rules. Would old Slysaw come down after them? Likely he would, if the stairs were passable. She considered for the first time that the creature, whatever it was, might have cut the stair root, eaten the stairs themselves. In which case, Slysaw couldn't follow, and where would their proof be then? And Mercald might be permanently out of his head, in which case they didn't have a judge. So, so, "Gamelords," she swore fervently.

The sounds from below grew louder, even as the light around her grew dimmer, more watery. Now it was dusky, shadowy, an evening light. She searched the darkness below her for lights, lanterns, torches, seeing nothing. She looked up at the wall once more, watching it float past, thinking.

She had to think about Roges. Roges, by the Boundless. A Maintainer. Though she knew some Bridgers who were married to Maintainers. Several of them. Quite happily. Rootweaver herself had been married to a Maintainer, so it was said. He had been killed during a storm, a great storm of rain which had almost drowned Topbridge and all who lived there, but he had saved Rootweaver's life, so it was said. She recalled what Roges had said. "We are more than servants, much more." That was true. It wasn't always remembered, but it was true.

"Beeeedieeee," came a call from below. Roges' voice again. She looked down, seeing the lights now, glowing fish lanterns making green balls of lights, yellow and blue balls of light all along the bridgetown mainroots, two glowing necklaces of lights in the depths. She was not quite above the town, and for a moment she felt panic, believing she would fall on past, but then there was a brush of wings and a voice, "Well, sausage girl. You and Mercald are the only ones I've had to fish in. Roges and the whatsit fell straight as a line. Hold on, now, I'll tow you a little. . . ." Her straight line of fall turned into a long, diagonal drop that brought her over the open avenue of Bottommost.

"I'll not appear like this," Mavin called in a whisper from above. "Join you later. . . ."

The bridge grew larger, larger, more light, more sound, wondering faces looking up, a great tangled pile of flattree leaves below with Roges reaching up from the middle of it, reaching up, to grab her—then they stood together as the leaf fell over them, closing them in a green fragrant tent, away from the world. He was holding her tightly. She was not trying to get away. Neither of them were saying anything, though there was much chatter from outside.

Mercald was saying, "Get them out from under there before they suffocate," and Beedie was thinking quietly that she would like to suffocate Mercald and to have done it yesterday. Then the leaf was pulled away amid much shouting, and Roges untied the lines from her waist.

"I'll save the cord," he said in a strangely breathless voice. "We'll need it later, I don't doubt."

She needed to say something personal to him, something real. "The fall—I was scared. When I jumped, all of a sudden, I was really frightened."

He looked at her with a kind of joyousness in his eyes that she didn't understand at all. "Were you really, Bridger? So was I." Then Mavin in her persona of bird-woman came calmly through the crowds and the moment's understanding was behind them.

"Come on," she whispered. "Though I must pretend to be the birdwoman once more, I have serious need of breakfast, and tea, and a wash. And poor Mercald needs a change of clothing. Unfortunately for him, his unconscious state did not last until he landed. And then we all need to revise some plans, or make some. It seems things are worse than we knew."

They had landed just outside the Bridgers House of Bottommost. It was a small house, not as well kept as the one at Topbridge, but with a guest wing, nonetheless, though one barely large enough for all five of them.

After a quick wash, they went along to the House dining hall, Mercald resplendent in his robes and hat—the only garb he had to wear while his others were being washed. As for the rest of them, they were only cleaner, not otherwise changed except that Mavin was once more playing her silent role of birdwoman. The food was quickly provided and almost as quickly eaten before Roges and Beedie were taken aside into a smaller room where the eldest Bridger of Bottommost awaited them, wringing his hands and compressing his lips in an expression of concern.

"The Messenger came yesterday, Bridger. We did not expect you for many days still, and yet here you are! I thank the Boundless you have come, for it was only two days ago we first saw the *thing*. I have sent word to the head of chasm council, but we cannot expect a response from old Quickaxe—or from his junior, Rootweaver—for some days.''

"By *thing*," said Beedie, "I suppose you mean the gray monster with the oozing hide." At his expressions of awed dismay, she went on, "We encountered it on the downward stair. Eating the stair, I should say. Just the other side of Nextdown.''

"Is it true what my Bridgers say?" the old man asked, hoping, Beedie knew, that she would say it was all an exaggeration.

"It is a thing some six or seven man heights long, as big around as this room, Elder. A . . . man who is with us says he believes it is sick. He believes it has been poisoned, perhaps purposely, by . . . Roges, what can I say? By what?''

"By people, Beedie. The . . . ah, the messenger of the Boundless who is with us says that there may be . . . people in the depths. That is, if it was not done by people from this town, Elder.''

Beedie sighed. "Elder, have you made any attempt to kill this thing? Or have you had any word of any intelligent creatures living below you in the depths?''

"Never." He wriggled the thought around in his mouth for a time, trying it between various pairs of teeth, finally spat it back at them. "No, never. As for killing the thing, I would not know where to begin. As for the other, my Bridgers go down the roots as Bridgers do, and up, and out across the root wall. We see the usual things. Crawly-claws. Slow-girules. Wireworm nests, sometimes. Leaves fall from above, and sometimes the nets of Topbridge or Nextdown miss them so we catch them. It is true that the Fishers bring up strange things from time to time, oddities which we cannot explain. But intelligence below . . . well, I've never heard any allegation of it.''

"The lost bridge?" prompted Beedie. "That would be below you, wouldn't it?''

"Oh, but my dear Bridger. What is the lost bridge? Sometimes I wonder if it ever existed! And if it did, is it not surely gone? No one has seen or heard of the lost bridge for what?—hundreds of years."

She shook her head. "When there was a lost bridge, before it was lost, Elder, how did people get to it? Was there a stair?"

He made a face at her, age grimacing at the silly ideas of youth. "There is said to have been a stair. Yes. At the morning-light side. We even have some books with adventure tales for children concerning the stairs and the lost bridge and all the rest of it. Would you like to see them?"

Beedie started to say no, indignantly, then caught sight of Roges' face, intent upon the old man's words. "I would, yes, Elder. If you would be so kind."

"I will have them sent to the guest rooms. Have you any other word for me, Bridger? We are very much afraid of these creatures. . . ."

"They are afraid of fire," said Beedie firmly. "It is thought they might be afraid of light."

"Not of our lanterns, I'm afraid. The one we saw two days ago was on the stair trail which leads to the mines below Miner's bridge. It is a little used way, built for the convenience of the Miners, to bring loads of some materials across to us for processing. It was lit by fish lanterns, and the thing had eaten great pieces of the stair, lanterns and all, when first we saw it. Fire—that's a different thing. Torches. We do not often use torches. It is damp this far down in the chasm. Except during the wind, smoke lies heavy upon Bottommost. Still, if fire will drive the monsters away, we must somehow learn to use fire once more. . . ." And the old man turned away, weary and fearful, yet somehow resolute.

They walked back toward the guest rooms, Beedie's hand finding Roges' as they went, silent, dismayed not a little. They slipped into the room Mavin shared with Beedie and told her what had transpired.

"So the Thinker was right," said Mavin. "The things have only recently been seen so far up in the chasm.

Well, they must somehow be made to go back where they have been. We will stay here in Bottommost today, perhaps tonight. Read the books when they are brought, sausage girl.'' Then, seeing her annoyed expression, "Read them to her, Roges, if you will. I will return after dark. If anyone asks, the messenger of the Boundless is asleep,'' and she slipped out of the room, disappearing down the corridor.

"Do you want to sleep, too?" asked Roges. "Our rest last night was interrupted."

"Later perhaps. Not now. Now I want to see Bottommost, the mysterious bridgetown I have heard of since I was a child! Aunt Six says it is all rebels and anarchists here, that there is no custom worthy of the name, that bad children gravitate to Bottommost as slow-girules to root mice. We are here and I must see if she lied to me."

They left Mercald curled up on a clean bed, quietly asleep. They left the Thinker sitting in a window, staring at nothing, a small muscle in his left cheek twitching from time to time. Beedie had had the generous intent of asking him if he wanted to go with them. One sight of him changed her mind. The two of them went out together, out of Bridgers House onto the main avenue of Bottommost.

"It's narrow!" she exclaimed. "It's little." Compared to Topbridge, it was narrow and confined, the lines of lanterns which marked the mainroots only two hundred paces apart, beads of light softly glowing in two arcs that met at the far wall. "And it's like nighttime!" Far above them the light of the chasm could be seen as a wide line of green, slightly shifting, as though they looked upward into a flowing stream, but the light upon the bridge came more from the ubiquitous fish lanterns than from the sky. Every corner carried at least one of the scaled globes; every market stall was lined with them, blue orbs and green, with an occasional amber one here and there. Those which were amber, Beedie noticed, bore horns and warts and protuberances of various shapes and kinds as well as a discouraging set of fangs. "I would not like to be the Fisher who caught one of those," she remarked to Roges.

Bottommost was quieter than Topbridge. It buzzed with a muted sound, as though it did not wish to attract attention to itself. The cries of the hawkers were melodious and soft, a kind of repetitive song. "They don't look like rebels and anarchists," said Roges. "They look rather sad."

"It's because there's so little light. It's an evening sadness, a perpetual dusk. If I lived here, I would cry all the time." The colors of the place were strange to her high chasm eyes. Soft greens and grays and blues. No white or red, no yellow. "Look how narrow their nets are." The nets on either side of the railing were mere handkerchiefs, of no extent.

"Look up and you'll see why," murmured Roges. High against the light were the twin bars of Topbridge and Nextdown, bracketing Bottommost on each side. "If the nets were any wider, they'd be catching all the fall-down from up there. Not very pleasant for the net cleaners."

"Well, there's got to be *something* good about the place. Let's try a teashop." And in the teashop they began to appreciate the true flavor of Bottommost as the calls of the hawkers, the bells in the Birders House, and the soft light blended into music. If there were rebels in Bottommost, they were rebels of an odd sort, rebels of silence, of shadow, of gentle movement. "I haven't seen any Banders," she said. "None in the House."

"There are some here," he replied. "I asked the Maintainer who brought us blankets whether there had been any unrest on Bottommost concerning the messenger of the Boundless. She said yes, rumor and storytelling, a small attempt to whip up frenzy, resulting in nothing much. Still, there are some of them here, enough to do us any harm if we are not careful."

"Enough to carry the word back to old Slysaw?"

"I should judge so." He did not sound as though he cared greatly about it, about anything. He had been sitting, sipping, smiling at her for hours. She blushed. She, too, had been sipping, smiling. Resolutely, she got to her feet. "Roges. We promised Mavin we would read the books about the lost bridge." She took his hand, dragged him upright.

They went out onto the avenue, still hand in hand, lost in the gentle music of Bottommost, to remember it always as magical and wonderful, more wonderful than any of the truly wonderful things which were to follow.

Chapter 7

Lantern-eyed, fluff-winged she flew along the root wall, soft as down, observant as any owl in the dusk, peering at this, that, the other thing. There were many small creepies, many larger ones as well—claws gently waving, and things that came to the claws thinking they were something else; shelves of fungus in colors of amber and rose, washed into grays by the green light; other fungoid growths hanging upon the roots themselves in pendant fronds, projecting horns and antlers and mushroomy domes, pale as flesh, moist as frogs.

There was a chorus of smells, rich and fecund stenches, rot and mildew and earthy green slime. There were greens innumerable, bronzy green and amber green and the blue-green of far seas not remembered by the people in the chasm. The air was wet, wetter the lower she went, full of mist wraiths which seemed in any instant almost to have coherent shape. Her wings were wet and heavy, and she changed the structure of her feathers to shed the damp, bringing a clear set of membranes across her eyes at the same time.

Those who might have known her in the white bird shape would not have known her in her present form, and she took pleasure in this, in this renewed feeling of anonymity, of remoteness. Beedie was a good girl; Roges a treasure; the theoretician an interesting find; Mercald a necessary burden—and not good enough to be a partner for Handbright as she had been, though perhaps better than one could have expected for Handbright as she was now—but there was much to be said for solitude. There was time for contemplation, time for feeling the fabric of the place, time for memory.

There had been another place, not unlike the chasm in its watery light, a pool-laced forest, green under leaves, full shadowed in summer warmth and breathless with flowers. Mavin had come there in the guise of a sweet, swift beast, four-legged and lean, graceful as the bending grass. It had been a shape designed for the place, needful for the place, and her body had responded to that need without thinking. So she had wandered, unaware she was observed, unaware until she came one dawn to the shivering silver pool and saw her own image standing there, head regally high, crowned with a single spiraled horn like her own, male as she was female, unquestionably correct for that place, that time, without any requirement for explanation.

And there had been a summer then, without speech or thought or plan for the morrow; a summer which spun itself beneath the leaves and over the welcoming grass, sparkling with sun shards and bathed in dew. Morning had gone into evening, day into day, as feet raced upon the pleasant pastures and across the mysterious hills. And then a day, a day with him gone.

She had never named him in her mind, except to believe that whoever he was, he was Shifter like herself, for there was no such supernally graceful beast in the reality of this world, had never been, probably now would never be again. And when a certain number of days had gone without his return, she had Shifted herself and left the place behind her, sorrowing that she would not know him again if she met him in a street of any town or upon the road to anywhere at all. Outside of that place, that stream-netted garden of gold-green light, what they had been together would have no reality.

It was the sight of Roges' face that had made her think of this, Roges' face as he brooded over Beedie who, though she was beside him, did not see the way he looked at her. In that silken, passionate look which reverberated like soft thunder was what she had felt in the summer garden. And it made her think of something more, of that same expression seen fifteen years before on the face of the Wizard Himaggery. *Twenty years,* he had said. Return to him in twenty years. Over three-quarters of that time was gone. Well, she could not think of that now, not with Handbright's child soon to be delivered, and Mavin soon to take it away to be safely reared as a Shifter's child should be reared—not with the chasm to be explored—and all these lands beyond the sea.

She moved out into the chasm, away from the root wall, attracted by a hard-edged shape which spiraled down toward her. It was one of the rigid frameworks webbed with flopperskin which the Messengers used to fly between bridgetowns, gliding on the warm, uprising air to carry messages from Topbridge to Harvester's. She flew close, wondering what brought a Messenger to these depths.

It was no Messenger. The kite held a young man's body, shrouded in white upon the gliding frame, staring with unseeing eyes into the misty air. There were embroidered shoes upon his feet, a feathered cap upon his head, and his hands were tied together before him with a silken scarf. Someone had decked the beloved dead for this last flight. Someone had set dreams aside, love aside, to grieve over this youth, and in that grieving, had realized there would be no more time in which to dream.

She flew aside, eyes fixed upon those dead eyes, as though she might read something there, accompanying the body down as it fell, turn on wide turn into the narrowing depths. At last she let it go, watching as it twirled into the chasm, softly as a leaf falls, the bright feather upon the cap catching at her vision until it vanished in mist.

No more time in which to dream. Twenty years. The bird body could not hold the pain which struck at her then, a shiver of grief so great that she cried out, the sound echoing from root wall to root wall, over and over again, in a falling agony of sound. She did not often think of herself as mortal.

"I will return," she promised herself. "I will return."

And was Himaggery still alive in that world across the sea? Must be, her mind told her sternly. Must be. I would have known if anything had happened to him. I could not have failed to know.

There, in the chasm mists, the Mavin-bird sang its determination and decision, even while it sought for mystery in the chasm with wide eyes.

Back in the guest rooms of Bridgers House, Roges lay with his head in Beedie's lap and read to her.

" 'In the time of the great builders, the outcaste Mirtylon (he whose name came from the ancient times above the chasm) took captive the maiden daughter of the designer of Firstbridge, the Great Engineer, she whom he called Lovewings after the love he bore her mother who had died. For the Great Engineer had forbidden his daughter to marry Mirtylon, though he had sought her in honor and in love, for the Great Engineer feared to lose her from his house.

" 'And Mirtylon fled from the wrath of the Great Engineer, into the bottomless depths of the chasm, root to root, with his followers, losing themselves in the shadowy lands beneath the reach of the sun. Then it was the Great Engineer wept and foamed in his fury, for taken from him was what he held most dear in all his life, for Lovewings had gone with them. And he fell into despair. And in his despair he failed to set the watch upon the bridge, and in the night the great pombis came, lair upon lair of them out of the darkness, driving the people of Firstbridge down into the chasm to the half-built city of Secondbridge, called by some Nextdown. And though many came there for refuge, the Great Engineer was slain together with the Maintainers of his house.

" 'But unknowing of this was the outcaste Mirtylon and unknowing of this was Lovewings—who would have been greatly grieved, for she loved her father—so she married Mirtylon of her own will and lived with him in a cave at great depth upon the root wall while those who followed him drew great mainroots together for the establishment of the town of Waterlight. In those depths the light was that found deep in river pools of their former lands, mysterious and shadowy. And in time the bridgetown of Waterlight was built, and Bridgers were sent from it to build a stair along the morning-light wall which should reach from Waterlight upward to the rim of the chasm. And in time the Bridgers so sent met the Bridgers of Nextdown upon the root wall, and the news of the death of the Great Engineer, her father, came to Lovewings.

" 'Then did she feel great guilt and great despair, accounting herself responsible for what had occurred, for she well knew with what value her father had held her. And she went to Mirtylon and told him she would go away for a time, to expiate her guilt in loneliness after the manner of her religion, but he would not let her go.

" 'And by this time the stair which Mirtylon had ordered to be built stretched upward from the depths into the very midst of the chasm, to the new-built bridge of Bottommost. Forbidden to expiate her guilt Lovewings took herself to the highest point which had yet been built and threw herself into the depths so that none saw her more. This is the story told of her, for none knew the truth of it save that she had climbed the stair and came no more to Waterlight.

" 'And Mirtylon despaired, ordering that the stair be shattered, that none might walk that way again. So it was broken, and all connection between Waterlight and the other cities of the chasm was cut off.

" 'Still the Messengers flew between the bridges, and there was trade of a kind between them, with much gathering of gems and diamonds from the Bottom lands by those of Waterlight, and much trading of this treasure for the foodstuffs which grew high above. And though the people of the bridgetowns were curious as to the source of the treasure, the secret was well kept by the people of Waterlight who would say only that the treasure was gathered at great danger to themselves from that which dwelt in the Bottomlands below.

" 'Until came a day the Messengers flew to Waterlight to find it gone, its place empty, the roots severed, the people gone, all in one night, vanished as though taken by a Demon or devil of the depths.

" 'And of Mirtylon many songs are sung, and of Lovewings, and of the vanished bridge which is called Lostbridge, and of the shattered stair. . . .'

"And that," Roges said, "is that. There's another story here about Lovewings. You want to hear it?"

"No," said Beedie definitely. "It's depressing. All that guilt and foolishness and throwing themselves about. I would like to know where the bridge went, though."

"So would Mavin," said Roges. "And I doubt not she'll find out, one way or another. Whatever she may be, she is very positive about things. I wonder who she is—what she is. . . ."

"I don't know. She's like the birdwoman. I mean, there are two of them, sisters. That's all I know. When I think about how she came when I was caught on the root, dying in the smoke, I know I should be frightened of her. But I'm not. She's just not scary."

"I think she's scary." Roges was serious, worried. "Though I try not to show it. She knows things. That's scary."

"Oh, the theo . . . theor . . . the whatsit knows things, too. And I know things. And some are the same things, and some are different things. That's all. It doesn't matter to *her*! It shouldn't matter to you."

Roges laughed, burrowed the back of his head into her lap, reached up to touch her face. "Beedie, you don't have any doubts at all, do you?"

"Hardly any," she agreed, in surprise that he should ask. "It seems an awful waste of time. You just do things, and if it doesn't work, then you do something else next time. Sitting around having doubts is very wasteful. At least, it seems so to me."

"Don't you ever worry about whether things are right or wrong?"

"Daddy and mum taught me what wrongs are. I don't do wrongs. I take care of my tools, and I don't risk my neck on the roots, and I'm castely in my behavior—mostly—and polite to my elders. I don't tell lies. What else would you like to know about me?"

"Are you religious?"

"Oh, foof, Roges. You know I'm not. Just enough to make sort of the right responses to noon prayers, and that's about it. Are you?"

"Some," he admitted. "I wonder about the Boundless a lot."

"Maybe you should have been a Birder."

"Maybe I was born a Birder. No one knows. I was found on the root wall, a foundling."

"Oh, Roges. That's very sad. Why, do you suppose?"

"I don't know. Never knew. Tried not to wonder."

"I'm sure I know," she said, grinning at him, not letting him see she was beginning to tear up again. "You were so beautiful a baby that everyone looked at you all the time. Your aunt had an ugly baby no one ever looked at, and it made her so jealous that she stole you away from your mum and daddy and hid you on the root wall, giving out the slow-girules had carried you away. And ever since then they've been longing for you, unable to find you at all."

"Not very likely," he said. "They'd have found me by now."

"That could be true. Well then, we'll say they got very sick from their loss, and they both almost died from despair. And their elders told them they had to give the mourning up."

"Now who's making stories about guilt and

despair?'' he asked her in mock fury. "Beedie. You're a crazy child."

"I'm not a child," she said, suddenly deciding it was time to prove it to him. "Not a child at all."

They were interrupted by Mavin's voice from the doorway, warm and amused. "I see I interrupt. Well, such is my fate. I have found the broken stairway, young ones." They turned to her, a little dizzy and unaware, not believing her at first, faces questioning. "True! Surprisingly, it is still there. Nothing has eaten it. It hasn't rotted. It is hatcheted away at the top end, but the rest of it goes down and down—overgrown a little, true—into the very depths."

Then they were both on their feet, the books—and other things—forgotten for the moment. "Did you go to the Bottom? Have you seen it? Shall we go now?" asked Beedie, ready as ever for action.

"I saw only a little. The light is scant enough at this depth, and what is there is waning. I think we will go at first light tomorrow. While I saw no signs of the gray oozers on the morning-light wall, it should be easier to avoid them in light. So. Let us go in light, such as it is." And she stretched herself upon the bed in the room. "Go on with whatever you were doing. . . ."

"Oh, Mavin," Beedie growled. "You are not always very funny."

"Not always," agreed Roges in a wry voice. "I think it would be a good idea for all of us to get some rest and a good meal here at Bridgers House tonight." He took up the books, placing them in a neat stack on the table beside Mavin's bed.

Mavin leafed idly through one of the books, scanning a few pages while Beedie talked about the story of Lovewings and Mirtylon and how sad it was, then let her eyes close.

"Mavin . . . Mavin. Are you asleep?"

"Trying very hard to be, sausage girl."

"Do you think old Slysaw is still following us?"

"I can guarantee he is, child. At this moment, he is two-thirds of the way down the stair to Midwall. He will rest in Midwall tonight. Two nights hence he will rest here in Bottommost. And the day after that, someone will show him where the broken stair is.''

"Do you think we will get proof he killed my family? That he set fire to the mainroot?''

"I don't think it matters, root dangler. Whether we get proof Mercald would accept or not, I have enough to suit me. You may depend upon it. Old Slysaw Bander will not return from the depths.'' And then there was only the gentlest of snores, like a dragon purring, as Mavin slept.

There was a traverse of considerable extent across the root wall between the morning-light end of Bottommost and the place the old stair began, its splintered end well hidden behind a cluster of side roots and a fountain of fungus. The Bridgers of Bottommost were so excited at the thought of finding the old stair, however, that they had worked most of the night while the expedition slept to build a temporary footbridge across the root wall. Except for Mercald, the expedition crossed it without difficulty, and Roges solved the Mercald problem by carrying him over on one shoulder. Once the stair was reached and they had burrowed into it with hatchet and knife and much flinging aside of great blobs of fungus, Mercald was able to stand once more, though it took him a little time to be steady on his feet.

"It's hidden," Beedie said, looking down the stair in the direction they would go. "The roots have grown all over the outside of it." Indeed, it was like walking through some dusky cloister, the roots on the outside of the stair making repeated windows into the chasm so that they walked first in shadow, then in half light, then in shadow once more. "How far down does it go, Mavin?"

"I didn't find out. Just found that the stair was here, then flew up above to check out old Slysaw. Shh. Here's the Thinker coming along behind. I'd as soon not talk with him about my private habits. Hush now."

They set a slow pace at first, warming up to it as the

day warmed, easing up again when they had eaten their midday meal, then slowing still further when the afternoon wind began to blow down the canyon, whipping the root hairs over the stairs, making their eyes water.

"I postulate a desert at the lower end of this chasm," said the Thinker, wiping his eyes so that he could see his notebook. "Quite large, very dry, very hot. At the upper end of the chasm a range of mountains, perhaps a tall, snow-capped range. . . ."

"Actually," said Mavin, "it's a glacier. A monstrous big one."

He did not ask her how she knew, but simply plunged on with his explanation. "The sun heats the air over the desert. It rises. The air in the chasm, being cooler, flows out onto the desert. The air over the glacier, being cooler still, flows down into the chasm. We have wind each day from afternoon through about midnight, by which time the desert has given up all its heat. Then the hot springs in the chasm begin to warm the chasm air once more. The lower we go in the chasm, the stronger the winds will become. That is, unless there are many barriers down there, narrowings, turns, fallen rock. In that case, it might be strongest above the bottom. . . ."

"Is that true?" Beedie whispered to Mavin. "Is that really why the wind blows every day? The Birders say the Boundless does it to move the smoke away, so we won't suffocate."

"Is there any reason it couldn't be both?" laughed Mavin. "I suppose the Boundless can use deserts and glaciers to sweep smoke away if it wants to."

"The way I would use a broom," said Roges. "Why not. Still, it makes traveling difficult." He wiped away a clot of wet root hairs the wind had driven into his face. "It wasn't this strong on Bottommost."

"It was stronger than you felt. The buildings on Bottommost are all built facing down-chasm, away from the wind. Besides that, they're all built with curved backs, I noticed, and there are wind shields along the streets." Mavin leaned out into the chasm to look down. She was now the only one of the party not constantly wiping streaming eyes, though the others had not noticed the clear lids she had closed to protect her own eyes from the wind. "We may have to find a sheltered place and wait until the wind drops before we go on. I've brought fish lanterns, so we needn't camp in the dark. Hss. What's that?" She pointed away along the root wall, toward a distant shadow. Roges and Beedie thrust their heads out, drawing them in immediately.

"I can't see anything," Roges complained. "What did you think it was?"

"A shape," she replied, still peering into the chasm. "Only a shape. Vaguely manlike. Perhaps it was nothing, only a shadow."

"Probably just a shadow. Our eyes are tired. I think stopping for a time would be a very good idea," said Mercald apologetically. "We've been climbing down since early this morning, and my legs have cramps in them. Both."

"Well then, why not. Start looking for some kind of declivity or protected spot. We'll stop as soon as we find one." Mavin drew her head in and clumped along behind them, her face both thoughtful and apprehensive.

Beedie moved ahead, Roges close beside her, searching the root wall. There were many small holes, but none large enough to offer shelter to the group. Then they came to a fairly flat stretch of stair solidly overgrown on the chasm side with only a shrill shiver of wind entering from the bottom end. "We could close that off," said Beedie, measuring it with analytical eyes. "I can cut some short lengths of ropey root, and weave a kind of gate across it, then we can put a blanket or two across it to shut out almost all the wind." Without waiting for the others, she began to hack at the wall, pulling down lengths of shaggy root. Roges tugged them to the opening, thrust ends into the root wall and began weaving them together, hauling and tugging until the woven gate was in place.

By this time the others had arrived, and Mavin fastened her blanket to the gate, tying it along the sides. It felt as though the temperature on the stair went up at once, just from excluding the cold wind.

"I suppose it would be too much to hope for that there'd be some deadroot along here," Mercald commented. "I'm thirsty for tea."

There was usually deadroot up under the thatch along the wall, and a few moments' scratchy burrowing brought a pile of it to light. It was brittle enough to break and dead enough not to threaten them with lethal smoke, but it was soggier than they were accustomed to burning. Roges had trouble lighting it upon the portable hearth. However, once started, it burned readily enough, the smoke roiling upwards along the stair. They sat in the firelit space, hearing the wind howl outside, all of them aware of some primitive, fearful feelings concerning darkness and the creatures which dwelt in it. Mavin found herself listening to the wind, listening through the wind, trying to hear what other sounds there might be in the chasm. There had been a manshape upon the root wall, and yet not exactly a manshape. It should not have been there. There were no men in the bottoms. She knelt, thrust her ear against the root stair, but there were no hostile sounds, no rasp of great slug teeth, only the thrumming of the wind upon the root fibers, the monotonous hum of steadily moving air.

They sat, dozed, woke with a start only to doze again. The light faded and Mavin took the fish lanterns out of her basket to hang one upon the staff she carried, one upon Mercald's staff. The light was not the warming amber-red of firelight but the chill blue-green of water, and they found themselves shivering.

"The wind will let up about midnight," said Mavin. "I suggest we wrap up tightly, get as close together as possible to share warmth, and wait until then to go on." She heard no dissent, not even from the Thinker, though he did not lie down among them but sat under the chill green lanterns muttering to himself, making notes in his little book.

The wind began to howl loudly, rocking the stair,

moving it in a curiously restful motion, so that they all slept as in a cradle, or, thought Mavin, as on the deck of a sea-going ship.

It was the cessation of motion that wakened Mavin, that and the stillness. The Thinker still sat, still muttered, eyes fixed on something the rest of them could not see. In the darkness, she could see firelight glittering on Beedie's open eyes.

"So. You're awake, sausage girl."

"I'm sore," she complained. "Next time I'm going to bring something softer to sleep on."

"How often do you plan to go on such expeditions?"

"Whenever I can. Don't you think it's exciting?"

"Umm," said Mavin. "What does Roges think?"

"I'm sure he thinks he'll be very glad when he can get me back to Topbridge and maybe marry me and probably talk me into having babies."

"What do you think about that?" Mavin sat back, pulling her own blanket around them so that they half reclined between Roges and Mercald, warmed by their sleeping bodies. "Is that something you would enjoy?"

"When Roges and I are—when we're . . . ah . . . involved, I don't mind the idea. Then, other times, like now, I *do* mind the idea. I want to go to Harvester's bridge and around the chasm corner and see what's there. I want to see that thing you told the Thinker about, that glacier. I can't do that if I'm all glued down on Topbridge with babies and Aunt Six being grandma. Whoof. I'd sooner eat dried flopperskin."

"By that, I presume you mean the idea lacks flavor."

"Flavor, and chewability, and a good smell. Oh, Mavin, I don't know. Were you ever in love?"

Mavin considered this. In the lovely summer forest, once, she had loved. In the long ago of Pfarb Durim, when she had been the age Beedie was now, she had looked into love's face, had heard its very voice. Since she had seen the dead youth fluttering like a dry leaf into the chasm, she had been aware of mortality in a way she had never been before. If she were honest, she would admit that the five years which stretched between now and that time she would meet Himaggery seemed a very long time, a time she would shorten if she could. And yet it would be hard to say why, for little had passed between them in that long ago time. Little? Or perhaps much?

Finally she answered. "I believe . . . believe that I love, yes. Someone. And yet, I have not sought him out in many years. I do not go to him or call him to me."

"How do you know he's still alive? People die, you know. Things happen to them." Beedie had thought of this in the night hours, had wondered how she would feel if she put off Roges until some future time and then found there was no future time for them. "If I had to choose, I suppose I'd rather have a child now than never do it at all."

Mavin shivered at this expression of her own thoughts. "You would rather love Roges now than never do it at all? Even though it might keep you from that far turn of the chasm?"

"Hmm. I think so. How do I know? Would there be someone else who would make me feel the same way? Would I have cheated him if I did not?"

Mavin chuckled, humor directed at herself rather than at Beedie. "I know. Since I met . . . the one I speak of, all other men have seemed to have . . . too much meat on their faces. I find myself longing for a certain cast of feature, a strong boniness, a wide, twisty mouth, eyes which seem to understand more than that mouth says. . . ."

"Eyebrows which meet in the middle over puzzled, sometimes angry eyes," whispered Beedie. "A certain smell to skin. A certain curl of hair around an ear. . . ."

"Ah, yes, sausage girl. Well, I will say only this one thing to you. If you would regret forever not having done a thing, then do it. But you need not give up your dreams in order to have done it. Go, if you will, and take your man and babies with you."

"Roges has the down-dizzies." She said it sadly, as though she had announced a dire and deadly disease.

"Well then, leave him at home with the babies and

tell him you'll see him when you return." She stood up, stretching her arms to hear the bones crack. "Midnight?" she announced loudly into the silence. "Are we ready to go on?"

They rose, groaning from the hard surface. "Stairs should be carpeted," said Beedie. "Either that, or they should put way stations with beds every half day along them."

"Shhhh." Mavin's hiss quieted them all. She had pulled the makeshift windshield aside and was leaning out over the stair rail, peering into the depths. "Look."

Below them in the suddenly calm air, the chasm was full of lights, globes of pearly luminescence which swam through the moist air, collected in clusters like ripening fruits, then separated once more to move in long, glowing spirals and curving lines. As they watched, several of the globes swam up to their level, peered at them from the abyss with wide, fishes' eyes from bodies spherical and puffed as little balloons of chilly light. One of them emitted a tiny, burping sound, then dropped with a sudden, surprised swoop to a much lower level and fled. The other, a smaller, bluer one, with quick, busy fins, followed them as they continued the downward way. There were smaller things in the chasm, also, vibrations of translucent wings, shivering dots of poised flight, darting among the glowing fish to be gulped down whenever they approached too near.

Other blue fish joined the one which followed them, and then still others, until they were trailed by a long tail of blue light, shifting and glowing. "There," said Mavin suddenly, pointing ahead of them. After a moment they saw what she had seen, huge stumps of mainroot, projecting into the chasm like broken corbels. "This is where the city was."

"*Waterlight*," said Beedie and Roges together.

"What was that?"

"Waterlight," said Roges. "The name of Lostbridge was really Waterlight. At least, according to the books up in Bottommost." ·

"I can see why," murmured Mercald. "I haven't seen

a bird of any kind since way before Bottommost. Do you think these fishes keep them away?"

"I think the air is too wet for them," said Mavin, not bothering to tell him that she knew so from experience. "Feathers would get soggy, heavy in this air. It would be almost impossible to fly."

"No Birders, then," he said. "I wonder what religion the people had to come uncomplaining into this depth."

"Follow the leader, I should think," said Roges. "The man who built Waterlight was named Mirtylon. From the tone of the stories we read, the people followed him and him alone."

"Always a mistake," said Mercald. "To follow men instead of the Boundless."

"On the other hand," remarked Beedie, "if you're following a man, he can at least tell you what he really expects you to do. Sometimes it seems to me the Boundless is a little vague."

Mavin was examining the end of the severed mainroots, noticing that they did not appear to have been chopped through or sawn. The ends were blunted, as though melted. She shivered. "Down," she said. "We're spending too much time in chitchat. This was the level of the city; now we'll find out where it went."

Though Beedie had expected the stair to end at the site of the ancient bridgetown, it went on down, doubling back on itself onto a new root system. They clambered around the turn, carrying the lantern fish which seemed to attract other, living ones, so that they continued to walk with a growing tail of lighted globes.

"Electron transport," said the Thinker suddenly, almost yelling. "Hydrogen segregation through cytochromes."

"What are you saying now?" asked Mercald in a kindly tone. "What is it, Thinker?"

"That's how they float. Hydrogen. They crack it out of water, using heme or hemelike proteins . . . remarkable." He did a little jig on the stairs, scratching himself as he sought his little notebook among his rags. "We could test it, of course. Try lighting one of them. It should go up in a puff of flame.''

"Difficult to light a flame down here, Thinker. Have you noticed how damp you are? How damp everything is?''

He had tried to separate the pages of his notebook which sogged into a kind of pulp in his hands, and he merely looked at her with an annoyed expression. Beedie felt the increasing weight of her hair, the knot on her neck as waterlogged as it was possible to be. Also, the air had grown warmer during the past hours so that they seemed to move through a thin soup, almost as much liquid as gas. "I've been in fogs as thick as this before,'' said Mavin, as though talking to herself. "But not many. I hope we're nearly down, for if it gets any thicker, we'll be swimming.''

She stopped, amazed, for the light of the fishes showed a net reaching out from the stair in every direction, as far as she could see on every side. Fish swam up and down through the meshes, some large, some small, and below the net they gathered by the thousands. The stair burrowed through the net, and they followed it down, silent, wondering, one man height, two, three, four. Then Mavin stepped off the root onto stone, the others crowding after. "Shhh,'' she said. "Listen. Water running.''

The sound seemed to come from all around them, a light splashing, babbling sound, an occasional whoosh of air, a chuckle as of streams over stone. "The fish are all above us now,'' said Beedie. "None below us. We must be at the Bottom.'' At that moment her feet struck solid stone.

"Look up,'' said Roges. "Noonglow.'' There, so far above them that it did not seem they could have come from that height, was the narrow ribbon of green light which meant noonglow, a mere finger's width shining through the fish-spangled gloom. "Bottommost is only a day and a half from the Bottom. I thought it was much farther than that.''

"No one has tried to find out for a very long time," said Beedie. "Because everyone believes it is dangerous. I told you that, Mavin."

"Indeed you did, root dangler. I haven't forgotten. But I remember also that you did not tell me why it is dangerous, or for whom. So—let us go carefully, watchfully."

"And well prepared," said Roges, taking his knife from his belt. "I thank the Boundless we have sure footing beneath us if danger comes."

"I, too," murmured Mercald. "I thank the Boundless for having seen such wonders. What must we do next?"

"The promise I made to Rootweaver, priest, was that we would put an end to whatever it is that eats the roots of the towns. So much; no less, no more. In return for which she keeps Handbright safe, awaiting our return. Well, we know it is the gray oozers which eat the roots. I have seen none of them on the root wall below Bottommost. So—I presume we must search." She had been speaking moderately loudly, loudly enough to attract a circle of curious fish, loudly enough that they were not really surprised to hear a voice answering her from outside their circle. . . .

It was a breathy voice, the kind of voice a forge bellows might have, full of puffing and excess wind. "You need . . . not search . . . far . . . travelers." The word was stretched and breathed, "*traaahvehlehhhrs*."

They turned as one, peering into the shadowy light, seeing nothing at first, locating the speaker only when it spoke again.

"What are . . . you looking . . . for . . . travelers? Is it . . . only . . . the bad beasts . . . of the . . . Bottomlands?" *Bhaaahtahmlahhhnds*?

Even Mavin, more experienced than the others in the variety of which the world was capable, shivered a little at this voice. There was something ominous in it, though the robed figure which stood in the shadows of the root wall did not menace them in any way. It merely stood, occasionally illuminated by a passing fish, its hood hiding its face. Mavin shivered again. "We do indeed, stranger. We seek certain beasts, if they are gray, and huge, and eat the roots on which the bridgetowns depend. And we are greatly surprised to find any . . . any person here in the Bottomlands, for we believed them occupied only by creatures. . . ."

"Ahhhh. But . . . you knew . . . of Waterlight." *Whaaaahtehr laihhht.* "Is it believed . . . "—puff, puff—"that . . . those on . . . Waterlight . . . perished?"

Beedie started to say something, but Mavin clutched her tightly by the shoulder, bidding her be silent. "Nothing is known of Waterlight, stranger. Nothing save old stories."

"Do the . . . stories . . . speak of . . . Mirtylon?"

"They do, yes," said Roges.

"I am . . . Mirtylon," *Aihh ahhm Muhhhrtihlohhn.* . . . said the figure, moving a little out of the shadow toward them, stopping as they took an involuntary step back, away from it. It was robed from head to toe in loose folds of flattree leaf; a veil of the same material covered its face; its hands were hidden in the full sleeves. It regarded them now through mere slits in the face covering, a vaguely manhigh thing, but with only a line of shoulder and head gleaming in the fish light to say that it had anything resembling manshape.

"Ah," said Mavin. "Waterlight has not been heard of for some hundreds of years. If you are indeed Mirtylon, then you have lived a long time, stranger."

"The . . . Bottomlands are . . . healthful. Things . . . live very . . . long here."

"Enzymes," murmured the theoretician, patting his pockets in search of the notebook which had turned to moist pulp. "Cell regeneration. . . ."

"We desire . . . to welcome . . . you . . . properly," the form went on. "Our . . . village is . . . only a . . . little distance, . . . toward the wind. . . ."

"One moment," said Mavin. "Let us confer for a time." She drew them into a huddle, watching the robed thing over Roges' shoulder. "There is something here I do not like," she muttered. "And I do not want all of us

in one heap, like jacks to be picked up on the bounce—
Aha, you play that game, do you? Well, I am not about
to have it played upon us.

"Beedie, I want you and Roges to go back up the
stairs, quick and hard. Keep going until you're *above*
where Waterlight used to be. Keep going until the air is
dry enough to get a fire going, then build a deadroot fire
on the hearth and keep it burning until you hear from
me. Don't let it go out. If anyone comes from above, it
will be Slysaw. Hide yourself and the fire as best you
can and let him come down. If anything comes at you
from below, use torches. Do not seem surprised at
anything I say, and do . . . not . . . argue with me!" This
last was at the rebellious expression on Beedie's face. "I
would send Mercald if I thought he could make the
climb fast enough. He can't. The Thinker would forget
what he was told to do in theorizing about something
else. I have no choice. Our lives may depend upon having someone up there who can go for help if we need it,
so get going."

Still resentful, Beedie turned toward the stairs, Roges
close behind.

"Surely . . . you will not . . . go so soon," puffed the
stranger. "We would . . . show . . . our . . . hospital . . .
ity."

"We have others waiting for us a little way up the
stairs," called Mavin, urging Beedie and Roges upward.
"I'm sending the young ones to bring them down. Can
you have someone meet the party here when they
return?"

There was a doubtful pause, almost as though the
figure engaged itself in conversation, for the figure
poised, bent, poised again in a way that had a questioning, answering feeling about it. Then at last the breathy
voice answered, "We will . . . meet them. Now . . . we
will . . . go to our . . . village."

Without looking back, the figure moved along the
chasm floor, winding its way between fallen rocks and
huge, buttress roots which emerged from the root wall
like partitions, ponderous in their height, thickly furred

with hair. Mavin looked up at the net spread above them, seemingly stretching from wall to wall of the chasm, from which more root hairs dropped into the rocky soil to make fringed walls along the path on either side.

"Protection," the Thinker muttered. "To protect them from stuff falling off the rim and from the bridgetowns. I would imagine the nets cover the entire area they occupy. And the net is living, of course, because of all these root hairs hanging down, which must mean that they cut these paths through it. No. No. Ah. Look," and he pulled one of the fringing root hairs up before Mavin's face. "Not cut. Rounded. As though it just stopped growing. Hmm. Now, what would make it do that. . . ."

Mavin did not answer. She was too busy considering that Mirtylon, seemingly so eager to offer hospitality, had not turned to see whether they followed. She looked behind her, seeking Mercald's face, pale as a fish belly. "Are you all right?"

"No," he whispered. "My heart is pounding. I smell something strange. It makes me sweat and shiver."

"Pheromones," said the Thinker. "Something exuded by a living thing to attract mates or warn predators away. Perhaps exuded voluntarily by some kind of water dweller. . . ."

"Perhaps involuntarily," murmured Mavin. "By something that calls itself Mirtylon."

Chapter 8

As they walked through the fibrous hallways of the Bottom following the robed stranger, Mavin felt all her senses begin to quiver and extend. Unseen by Mercald or the Thinker, she sharpened her eyes, enlarging them and moving them outward so that she could have a wider range of vision to the sides. What light there was was not much diminished by the netted roof they walked beneath for lantern fish swarmed through the whiskery jungle, casting pale circles of cold light.

Just above and slightly to her left, Mavin saw a hard-edged diamond shape upon the net, a thing of some weight, making the net sag beneath it. One of the rare amber fish nosed at the shape from above, and in that sunny glow she caught a glimpse of bright color, knowing it at once for what it was—the bright feather upon the cap of the young man whose body she had seen two days before, slowly circling upon its kite into the depths. The hallway led beneath it, and when she was almost below, she looked upward, quickly, to see the cap, the kite, the wrappings of white. There was no sign of the body which had been wrapped and decked in the clothes. She made no comment, merely trudged on, keeping close watch on the figure before her.

The sound of water grew louder, a bubbling and boiling with plopping heavings in it as of seething mud. They set foot upon a wooden bridge which led across this noise, through rising clouds of hot mist and the hiss of escaping steam. The bridge was made of short lengths of root, tied with bits of root hair to long, horizontal beams. The robes of the person before her moved in the rising steam without flapping loose, evidently being fastened at the ankle so that no surface of the body could be exposed. Mavin thinned her lips and marched on. Behind her the Thinker muttered once more about tectonics, rift valleys, plate separation. She had no idea what he was talking about, but naive intuition told her that the chasm Bottom burrowed near the great, hot heart of the world and was heated thereby. She needed no theorist's language to tell her that. Her own nose told her, full as it was of sulphurous, ashy stenches and the acrid smell of hot metal.

"We must . . . come to . . . shelter before the . . . winds begin," puffed their guide. "Else we . . . will be crushed."

"Crushed?" wondered Mavin. Certainly the winds were strong, but they had not been of crushing strength. What kind of creature might be crushed by such winds? She checked the two who followed, seeing them trudging along behind her, the one with his eyes fixed firmly upon his boots, the other staring placidly at everything he could see, muttering the while as though he stored away a million facts for later consideration. They had been walking for some time in a winding path that would have confused anyone other than Mavin. She had opened an additional eye in the top of her head and kept it fixed upon the green sky at the chasm top. Though they had walked a considerable distance, they had not come far from the stair. She estimated the distance Beedie and Roges might have climbed. They should be halfway back to the broken roots of Waterlight by now.

Keeping her eye fixed on their direction, she went on.

At a conjunction of the hairy hallways they found two other robed strangers waiting. One was silent. The other spoke in a manner no less breathy than the first, but with an unmistakably feminine voice, "We greet you . . . travelers. My name . . . is Lovewings."

Something tugged at Mavin's memory, an insistent, nagging thought which she could not take hold of. "It seems our arrival is not a surprise."

"You were . . . seen on the . . . Shattered Stair. No one has . . . climbed that . . . Stair for . . . a long time. The one who . . . saw you was . . . surprised. When we thought . . . about it . . . we knew it . . . must happen sometime. Sometime . . . bridge people must . . . come down." This short speech took an interminable, windy time. It appeared to have exhausted the speaker, and Mavin wondered if they ever spoke to one another in this watery depth or whether they communicated in some other fashion. Certainly their voices seemed unaccustomed to regular use.

"How long has it been since you had commerce with the bridgetowns?" asked Mercald.

"Since . . . since Waterlight . . . fell. Since then. Except . . . there have . . . sometimes been . . . people fall. Into the . . . nets." For all its breathiness, the voice was wistful. Why did Mavin distrust that wistfulness? Could it not reflect an honorable desire for company?

"Why did Waterlight fall?" demanded the Thinker. "Was it conflict? Rebellion? Something eating the roots?"

"Aaahhh," breathed the first guide.

"Aaahhh," echoed the second. There was silence, then the third figure spoke.

"It was . . . was the desire of . . . those on . . . Waterlight. To . . . to go into . . . the Bottomlands . . . and live there. . . ."

"In expiation for those who died on Firstbridge?" demanded Mercald eagerly. "Because of all the deaths that were caused then?"

"Oh, yes . . . yes," all three of the figures sighed, in

breathless unanimity. Suspicious unanimity, Mavin thought. They sounded like children caught in some naughtiness who seized upon an offered excuse with relief that they did not need to make up a story of their own. What was going on here? Was it so easy to put words into their mouths?

She spoke quickly. "You have lived here, then, since your scouts first explored here, before Waterlight was taken down. You took Waterlight down yourselves, of course, after you had moved here."

"Of course," sighed the breathy, male voice of the one who called himself Mirtylon. *Ahhhv cohhhhrz.*

"Of course," said the female voice, almost simultaneously.

So she calls herself Lovewings, thought Mavin. Lovewings. What was it she could not remember about Lovewings?

The beard-walled hallway opened into a larger space, a clearing near the morning-light wall through which a quick, cool stream ran down into the steamy lands behind them. Mavin's eye told her that she was only a few wing beats from the stair, though their pathway had wound back and forth across the chasm a dozen times in the last hours. A few score openings gaped in the chasm wall before them, carefully rounded, some of them decorated by a carved fretwork at the sides and top. Around each opening a cloud of fish lanterns hovered, nibbling at the fungus which grew there.

"Saprophytic," murmured the Thinker. "Living upon waste and decay, to be eaten in turn by the fishes, which may be eaten in turn by the occupants. Though I wonder if they would digest at all well? Phosphorous poisoning? I would need to look that up."

"Will you . . . enter?" the robed figures inclined themselves in a mere hint of bow. "Soon the . . . wind will . . . blow."

"My friends will stay here," said Mavin in a firm voice, "until I have seen whether these accommodations are suitable. Mercald? Thinker? Thinker! Can you concentrate on simply standing here for a few moments?"

She had succeeded in jolting his attention away from the lantern fish, at least for the moment. She walked up the little slope to the cave, giving no appearance of hurry or distress. The cave was shallow and sandy-floored with a hinged screen standing ajar. Not large, she thought. Large enough for the three of them to lie down in, not large enough for anyone else to come in. And not furnished with anything. Not a pot of water, not a rag to wash one's face, not the semblance of a chair or bed to soften the sandy floor.

She knelt, taking a handful of that sand in her fingers. It was dotted with bright, smooth stones which gleamed at her in blues and violets and greens. Gems. Some of them huge. They were not faceted, but smooth, as though worn by water. Looking back through the gate, she saw sparks of light thrown from many places in the clearing. Well now, she thought. That is interesting. No furnishings of any kind. But protected places, out of the wind. And gems. Everywhere.

"Very nice." She went out. "Very comfortable. Do come up, Mercald. Thinker. We offer our thanks, *Mirtylon*. And to you, *Lovewings*." The robed figures confronted her still, offering no food or drink, no comfort or company.

"Aaahhh," murmured the one.

"Aaahhh," echoed the others.

"We will find water when we need it in the stream, of course, and root mice growing upon the wall, and edible mushrooms. You mean us to take food and water as we need . . . of course."

"Of course," sighed the one.

"Ahhhv cohhhrz," echoed the others.

Mercald and the Thinker came in as Mavin pulled the gate across the opening and peered through it at the figures outside. For a time, they did not move. At last, the three turned away as though joined by invisible strings and moved across the clearing where they halted against the dangling root hairs and did not move again.

"You notice," Mavin asked, "no offer of food, or drink. No beds. No chairs."

THE FLIGHT OF MAVIN MANYSHAPED   143

"Persons living a life of religious expiation would hardly be expected to think of such things," said Mercald in a sententious voice. "It is likely that they fast for days at a time. Probably they engage in self-mortification as well, flagellation or something such, and robe themselves both to avoid licentiousness and to hide their wounds from one another's eyes."

"I don't know what they engage in, priest, but I do know that hospitality to strangers is a duty of every religion I have ever encountered with no exceptions. None. I am inclined to believe, therefore, that all your blather about expiation and fasting and what not is just that—blather. I don't know what's going on here, but it isn't religious."

"Besides which," said the Thinker, "it's unlikely that Lovewings, who committed suicide several hundred years ago, could be still alive. To say nothing of Mirtylon, who would have to have lived for about nine hundred years. Unlikely they would still have any licentiousness to cover."

"Of course!" Mavin struck her forehead with one hand, waving the other at the Thinker. "That story Beedie was telling me about the lost bridge. Lovewings was the one who threw herself off the stairs."

"The Boundless might extend the life of any worthy . . . " Mercald began, only to be cut off.

"The Boundless might, but I'll bet my socks the Boundless didn't. No, Mercald. Something other than the Boundless is at work here. Best rest while you can. They say they are concerned about the wind, and yet they stand out there in the clearing, not taking shelter. Something is awry here, so let us be cautious." She lay on the sandy floor, accommodating herself to it, placing her head where she could see through the woven gate, hearing Mercald burrowing in his pack, smelling the food he unwrapped but refusing a share of it when he offered.

The sides of the sandy clearing were hung with thick mats of root hairs, like the pelt of some giant beast, and against this shaggy background the robed figures stood out plainly, as silent and unmoving as when they had first arrived there. There were some dozen of the forms around the clearing, all standing with hooded heads slightly down, hands and arms hidden in the sleeves of the flattree-leaf robes. Mavin nagged at herself, wondering what was odd about the grouping, realizing at last that the creatures stood at strange, out-facing angles one to the other, not toward one another as people tended to do in groups. "Thinker," she whispered. "Look here."

When he lay beside her, she said, "Look at them. Are they talking with one another?"

He stopped breathing for a time, mouth half open around a chunk of cold fried root mice. Then he sighed. "No. Not talking. But something is happening. Look at the shifting, at the far end of the group, then the next one, then the next, as though they are moving slightly, one by one along that line. You don't think they are people at all, do you? Well. I have my doubts. We should see what's under those robes. Do you want me to postulate?"

"No. Better just find out what's under the robes. I'm going to sneak out, get around through the root wall. I think you'd better stay close to this cave, not wander about, and you'll probably be safer if you keep the gate shut until I return."

"The root hairs out there are impenetrable. The mean density of root hairs per square. . . ."

"Never mind," she said. "I'll manage." She pulled the gate open, slipped through and sidled along the root wall until her relocated eyes told her she was out of direct line of vision from any of the fretted arches. The group across the clearing still stood, heads down. She Shifted.

Spidery feet with sharp claws levered long legs up the rootwall. Spidery eyes, multifaceted, searched for any sign of movement. Once she had climbed above the level of the netted roof, she stopped to peer away toward the stairs, seeking upward for a fugitive gleam of light. There was still too much light in the chasm to tell whether it burned or not. She thought she saw a little, golden gleaming upon the wall but could not be sure. Well, that matter would wait. Both Roges and Beedie were sensible; they would not take chances.

The net bounced beneath her as she moved to the place the kite had rested. Once there she turned it over with angled legs, searching with mandible and claw. Only the wrappings, the clothing. Nothing else. Except —except a smell. A scent. Not unpleasant, but odd. Odd. Making her shiver and sweat. What was the word the Thinker had used. Pheromones? Well, and what was that? Stinks. Emitted by things. So, there were stink bugs and stink lizards and perfume moths. Back in the long ago, she had met an Agirule. It had had a strange, fungus smell, earthy and warm. Himaggery had smelled like autumn woods. Pheromones. So, these wrappings smelled like the creature that called itself Mirtylon. Which meant, so far as Mavin was concerned, that Mirtylon or one of his fellows had been here. And now the body of the youth was gone. Only his bravely feathered cap, his funeral wrappings remained. She shifted uneasily on her many legs, jigging upon the net until it quivered beneath her.

Then she made her way across the net until she was above the quiet forms where they stood, silent and un-moving.

The wind had begun to blow by the time she reached the place, moving very slowly. The only light lay high upon the evening-light wall, only the eastern end of Topbridge breaking the line of shadow, a hard, chisel shape against the glow. The other bridgetowns hung in darkness. Beneath the net the lantern fishes swarmed in their thousands, moving now toward the walls where they dwindled, diminished, becoming dark egg shapes fastened tightly to the walls. Beneath the net the robed forms stood as they had first arranged themselves, the robes flapping a little in the wind. Mavin lay upon the net, let her legs dangle through it, appearing to be only another set of skinny roothairs dangling into the clearing, invisible among countless others.

She took hold of a sleeve, pulled it gently, gently, tugging in time with the wind. It was fastened tight. She send an exploratory tentacle along it, not believing what she found. The sleeve had no opening. The two sleeves were joined at the ends. If there had been arms and hands in these sleeves, they had never been expected to reach the outside world.

Her tentacle dropped to the sandy floor, probed upward at the top of the clumsy shoe shapes. No opening. Shoes and robe were one. The thing was a balloon, all in one piece. On the net, Mavin snarled to herself, a small, spider snarl. Well and well, what was the sense of this?

The end of the tentacle grew itself a sharp, ivory claw and cut a slit in the robe, moving like a scalpel along one rib of the flattree leaf of which the garment was made. When the slit was large enough, the tentacle probed through.

After which Mavin lay upon the net in furious thought. Whatever she might have suspected, she would not have suspected this. She slid down a convenient root hair, spent some time exploring the area very carefully, with great attention to the boiling springs, then went back up onto the net, finding her way quickly from there back to the cave.

She paused before entering, searching the high wall for the gleam of amber light, sighing with relief when she found it unmistakably. So. Beedie and Roges were there, above harm's reach if Mavin had reasoned correctly. Above one harm's reach, she corrected herself. Slysaw would have reached Bottommost by now. On the morrow, he would come down the Shattered Stair. Well and well once more. After midnight, when the wind stopped, would be time enough to worry about that. There were other things to think of first.

She slipped inside the cave, pulling the gate tight behind her and taking time to lash it with a bit of thong. Evidently Mercald had ventured out, for there was a pot of steaming tea upon the sandy floor. She looked around for the fire, before realizing there was no smoke.

"I ventured just as far as that boiling spring," said Mercald in an apologetic tone. "The Thinker kept watch. It's only at one side of this clearing. We both wanted something hot. I thought you would, too."

Mavin listened to the wind rising outside and nodded. It had been sensible of him, she had to admit. If one set aside the man's fear of heights, he was brave enough for all ordinary matters. Wishing she could like him more, for Handbright's sake if for no other reason, she crouched beside the steaming pot and took the cup he offered. If one could not have fire, this would do. There was a long silence. At last she looked up to see both pairs of eyes fastened upon her and realized that they were waiting for her.

"Can you still see the figures out there?" she asked Mercald who was sitting near the gate.

He peered into the dusk, nodded. "The wind is fluttering them a little, but they still haven't moved."

"They aren't likely to," she said. "They're anchored to the roots. Besides, they're empty." She waited for expostulation, surprise. There was none.

"When Mercald went out for the water," said the Thinker, softly, "he said they looked like the cloak room at the Birders House. Hanging there. The minute he said it, I thought that's why they were left out in the wind—because there was nothing in them."

Mavin peered through the gate, head cocked to one side. They did have that look, a kind of limpness even though she knew they were supported from within by a framework of wiry greenroot.

"They are made like balloons," she began, going on to describe the framework of flexible strands inside, with the flattree leaves stretched over. "There are two slits in the veil, probably to appear as though the beings have eyes, but I doubt it. Then there are no soles to the shoe parts. There is a smell there, at the bottom of the things, as though something flowed out of them and along the soil, away into the root tangle. There are places along there where the roots don't reach the ground, places about ankle high and an armspan wide, where the roots look burned off or chewed off. No, the ends are smooth. They look—rounded, somehow."

"Digested off," suggested the Thinker.

"Perhaps," she agreed, sitting silent for a time after that trying to visualize a being shaped like a flatcake, with an odd smell, which could eat greenroot without dying from it. "Of course, once I saw the greenroot framework inside those things, I knew they couldn't have been people."

"It would poison people," agreed Mercald. Fresh greenwood sap on the skin, even small quantities of it, caused ulcers which did not heal. He had been listening to all of Mavin's discoveries, sadly shaking his head from time to time, not in disagreement but in profound disappointment that what he had thought was a religious community was likely to be something quite different.

"And then," she went on, "I found a burial kite—what do you call them?"

"Wings of the Boundless," said Mercald. "Which carry the dead into the Boundless sky. Or, sometimes, into the Bounded depths. Depending upon what kind of life they've lived, of course."

"Of course. Part of the duty of the Messenger caste, as I understand it? Manufacture of wings and dispatch of the dead thereon? Yes. Beedie told me. Well, two days ago I saw one of the . . . wings . . . descending into the chasm. There was a bright feather on the . . . well, on the fellow's cap. That wing now lies on the net a short way from here. The cap is there, and the white wrappings, and the other clothing, but the body is gone."

"Of course it's gone," said Mercald with asperity. "It went into the care of the Boundless."

"I thought the ones that went up went into the care of the Boundless. This one came down."

"Well, naturally, both end up in the care of the Boundless, it's just that . . . our . . . theology is a little indefinite about . . . "

"It's just that you don't know, Mercald. Do you

really think that the Boundless cares about bodies? Well, no matter. In my experience across the lands of this world, bodies invariably vanish because something buries them or burns them or eats them. Beetles, usually. Or things that look like beetles. Except that I could find no beetles around the kite. Excuse me, Mercald. Around the Wing of the Boundless.

"I did find the smell of whatever. Whatever wore those robes. Whatever greeted us in human language. Whatever guided us here. Whatever has now gone elsewhere, probably because the wind has started to blow and whatever is afraid of being crushed."

"The inescapable hypothesis is, then, *whatever ate the people of Lostbridge*," said the Thinker.

"Whatever," agreed Mavin. She leaned forward to fasten the rattling gate more tightly. The wind kept up its steady pressure on the thong, stretching it.

"How horrible," said Mercald, making a sick face. "How dreadful."

"Dreadful, certainly," she agreed. "But helpful. I think we can draw some conclusions from what we know, can't we, Thinker?"

"Ahhm. Well. Yes. A form of life which absorbs some—how much, I wonder?—of the mental ability *or* memory of whatever it eats. Hmmm. Yes. Language for example? Yes. Hmm. Doesn't manage it any too well, but does have the general idea. Tends to use it reflectively. . . ."

"They don't think very quickly," said Mavin. She had come to this conclusion some time ago. The poor creatures, whatever they were, did not think well. They struggled with thought, struggled to put ideas together, like a partly brain-killed Gamesman trying to do things he had once done easily, not able to understand why these simplicities were now impossible. She had seen that. More than once. She clenched her teeth at the memory, set it aside.

"What would explain this masquerade? Why the robes? Why the names of the long gone?"

Mercald cleared his throat. "Because, Mavin, they

told the truth when they spoke of expiation. No. Listen. Let us suppose these creatures, these whatever, came upon Waterlight in the darkness those hundreds of years ago, came upon it and ate the people, only to take into themselves all the memories of those people, and the thoughts, language, feelings. All the sorrows. All the pain.

"Before that, they had been animals. They hadn't had any 'thinking' at all. Now, suddenly, they would have language and thought and guilt. For the first time, guilt. Oh, what a terrible thing. A simple animal of some kind, with only animal cleverness or skill, and then suddenly to have all that thinking. No way to get rid of it. No way to go back as they were before. Only the idea of expiation which they had swallowed at the same time they swallowed guilt, but no way to do that, either. And the thinking perhaps gets less and less useful as time goes on. . . ." He fell silent, sorrowing, hearing the wind sorrowing outside as though it agreed with his mood.

"Probably asexual reproduction," said the Thinker. "Which means clones. Which means no change, no natural selection. Every generation the same as the preceding generation, and every individual—though there really wouldn't be individuals in that sense—the same as every other. So, whatever ate Mirtylon is still Mirtylon. And whatever ate Lovewings is still Lovewings. . . ."

"Because she didn't die when she jumped," said Mavin. "She landed in the net and the whatevers got to her while she was still alive."

"Possibly more than one of them," the Thinker went on. "And possibly learned from her that there was good eating on Waterlight bridge. If that was the case, then we have to assume that the total effect of thought didn't come about immediately. Maybe it took some time for it to be incorporated into the beings, the whatevers. . . ."

"Poor things," said Mercald, sadly. "Poor things."

"Well, if they are such poor things, tell me how to help them, Priest. Would you have them expiate, finally, what it was they did? Perhaps we could arrange it.

That is, provided they don't eat us first."

"Surely not. Having once felt guilt . . . "

"Having once felt guilt, Priest, there are those who court it, believing that more of the same can be no worse. No, there may be sneaky slyness at work here. I will believe only what these creatures do, not what they say. I do not think they understand words very well, though they use them. I have known people like that in the world above. They say human words, but from an unhuman heart. Even a thrilpat may speak human language, often with seeming sense, but that does not mean I would trust one with my dinner."

"But you speak of expiation. . . ."

"Yes. Something is trying to kill the oozers that threaten the bridgetowns, or so Thinker says. We know of nothing which could be making that attempt save these whatevers. So. If these creatures, whatever they are, succeed in killing the gray oozers, then they will have expiated their guilt at wiping out Lostbridge—Waterlight. We will give them . . . what is it you give penitents, Priest? Forgiveness? We will give them that. Perhaps it will satisfy them."

"Perhaps," agreed Mercald, giving her a narrow and suspicious look. "And do you intend to give them Slysaw Bander and his followers, as well?"

Mavin smiled a slow smile at him, a wicked smile which burrowed into him until he shifted uncomfortably, unable to bear the stare. "Well, Priest. I thought of it, yes. And I decided against it. Can you tell me why?"

He sighed in relief, wiped his forehead which had become beaded with perspiration. "Because you are a messenger of the Boundless, Mavin, and would not judge without proof?"

"No, Priest," she said in the same wicked tone. "Because I am a pragmatist. I do not want one of these whatevers sliding about in the Bottomlands with Slysaw's evil brain alive inside it, moving it. It may be we are fortunate that none of those who were eaten on Lostbridge desired power. If they had wanted power or empire, the creatures that ate them might not have stopped with Waterlight. If Slysaw Bander had eternal life, clone or no clone, I would not sleep soundly in my hammock anywhere in this chasm or, it may be, in this world. Even though the things seem to have trouble keeping their train of thought, I would not risk it. It may be they merely find language difficult.''

Mercald flushed. ''You mock me, Messenger.''

''I instruct you, Priest. Pay heed. When you believe that messengers arrive from God, it is wise to listen to everything they say, not merely when they recite accepted doctrine.'' She was ashamed of herself almost immediately. He turned so pale, so wan. Well. It was only as she had suspected from the beginning. Many men had a strong tendency to tell God how to behave, and religious men were more addicted to this habit than most.

''All of which,'' she said, changing the subject, ''is not relevant to our current need. We need a way to destroy the oozers. The whatevers evidently have not found a way, not yet. It would help if we knew whether the whatevers think at all. Do they think, Thinker?''

He shrugged. ''What is thought? No current theories explain it. I suggest you attempt what it is you wish to do and see whether it works. Though I am not an experimentalist, at times one must simply sit back and observe what experimentalists manage to accomplish. In the interest of acquiring data. No other way. Sorry. Sometimes, one simply must.''

''Well, then, Thinker, we are stymied until the wind stops. Whatever they are, they will not come out until midnight. I suggest we sleep until then, keeping watch turn about. Priest, you seem wide awake.''

''I am troubled,'' he said with dignity. ''I will watch first. It is unlikely I would sleep in any case.''

''I have abused you,'' said Mavin, ''if only for your own good. So watch then. Wake me when you grow sleepy.''

She curled into a ball on the sandy floor, covering herself with her blanket. Though the gate of the cave was loosely woven, it seemed to be out of the wind, protected on the up-chasm side by a protrusion of the root wall. The wind was cool but did not feel as cold as it had the night before upon the stair. She drowsed, half dreaming, half remembering.

Near the source of the River Dourt was a town called Mip. It lay in the valley of the Dourt, below the scarps of the Mountains of Breem, far east of the Black Basilisk Demesne of which the people of Mip spoke often, softly, and with some fear. As far to the east as the Black Basilisk lay west was the Demesne of Pouws, and between the two demesnes a state of wary conflict had become a way of life and death. Mip, lying as it did between, strove quietly to be invisible. The people around were small holders, farmers, those to the south raising livestock while those in the river valley grew vegetables and fruits for towns as far away as Vestertown and Xammer in the south or Leamer in the north. Thus the town itself was largely devoted to commerce of an agricultural kind, full of wagons and draft animals, makers of harness and plows, seed sellers, animal Healers and minor Gamesmen who would dirty their hands and Talents with ordinary toil.

Mavin had come there, pursuing the white bird, coming south from Landizot, down the rocky shores of the Eastern Sea, past Hawsport, with its harbor full of fishing boats behind the breakwater, down along the mountains to the Blask Basilisk Demesne which was mad with celebration over the birth of a boy child named Burmor to the family of the Basilisks. Mavin went quiet there, anonymous, answering fewer questions than she was asked, learning at last that the white bird had been seen. "Ah, yes, stranger. Seen by the Armigers on duty at the dawn watch. Two of them flew off in pursuit of it, losing it in the haze above Breem Mountains. It would have gone to water along the Dourt, no doubt. But that was some time ago. Ask in Mip."

So she had gone to Mip.

A quiet little town, on both sides of the Dourt, which so early in its flow was little more than a brook, full of inconsequential babble and froggy pools. A town full of trees, planted there, most of them, generations before by the first settlers in the area. "We feed the Basilisks," she heard whispered. "We feed Pouws. They have no wish to go hungry, so they leave us alone."

And, indeed, there was little sign of Great Game in Mip. No tumbled rocks to show that Tragamors had heaved the landscape about. No piles of bones to show where Gamesmen had pulled the heat from the very bodies of the townsmen to fuel their Talents. An occasional Armiger from the Black Basilisk Demesne high in the western sky, light shattering from his armor; an occasional highly caparisoned Herald from Pouws stopping for beer at the Flag and Branch on his way to or from some other place. Mavin had settled into the town, found a quiet room on the upper floor of the Flag and Branch and moved about to ask questions.

There was a hunter in Mip. "I saw the bird, Gameswoman, in the marshes. The source of the Dourt lies there in the ready marshes, and the wild fowl throng there between seasons, moving north or south. I did not attempt to take the bird. I do not take the rare ones. Only the common ones, those we may eat without feeling we have eaten the future and so kept it from the lips of our children. It seemed contented there, though without a mate or nest or nestlings to rear. If you go there, likely you will find it, though if you go to harm it, I would beg you to reconsider."

"I am a Shifter," Mavin had said. "As is the white bird. My sister."

At which the hunter had moved away, with some expressions of politeness, his face suddenly hard and unpleasant. It was not the first time Mavin had seen that expression when Shifters were mentioned. Seemingly no other Gamesmen—no, not even Ghouls and Bonedancers, who moved among hosts of the dead to the horror of multitudes—were held in such disrepute. It was not contempt. It was fear. Seemingly some pawns did not believe the carefully constructed mythology which Shifters were at considerable effort to put about.

Seemingly some pawns believed they had special reason to distrust, to fear the Shifter Talent. It was a reaction Mavin found curious. She promised herself she would learn the cause of it some day.

Come that day when it would come; she took herself off to the swamps at the source of the Dourt. This was high country, much wooded, with little meadows surrounding the streams and the low, marshy places grown up with reeds. It reminded her a little of another forested place, and she was almost contented there, in one shape or another, searching for the white bird.

The streams came down out of many shallow valleys into a myriad meadowlands. Searching was no matter of high flight and sharpened eyes. She had to seek along each separate creek and gully, among each separate set of marshes. It was not until ten days had passed that she caught sight of the bird, the white bird, helplessly beating her wings against the net which held her even as the hunter closed in to take her. If it was not that same hard-faced hunter she had left in Mip, it was his twin, and the anger that was always close to the surface in Mavin boiled up in a fury. Still, she held back, seeing the way he peered about, face sly and full of hating intensity. She knew then what he meant to try. This white bird, a Shifter, was to be bait for another Shifter, herself. The fact that he brought nothing but a net showed his ignorance. He believed, then, only the common knowledge about Shifters, much of it spread by the Shifters themselves. He thought a Shifter could be either human or one other thing—a wolf, a pombi, a fustigar, a bird.

"I am Mavin Manyshaped," she sang to herself in the treetop from which she watched him. "You have done a foolish thing, Hunter." Then she followed him as he put the white bird in a cage, a cage too small, painfully too small, and carried it away in a wagon.

Mavin, seeing him through flitchhawk eyes, circling high above him, saw each plodding step of the team.

He did not go far. Only to an open meadow where the white bird would be very visible for a long way, and there he tethered her tightly to a stake driven deep into the ground and set his nets to drop if that stake should be touched.

Mavin, watching him from mountain zeller eyes, merely smiled.

Dusk came, and after that darkness, and the hunter curled beside his dying fire to rest. What did he think? she wondered. Did he believe Shifters could not stay awake at night? Did he think that because one Shifter flew as a bird in the daylight that her sister would also fly only in the day? Foolish man. Her serpent's eyes saw him clearly by his warmth, even in the dark.

She slid beside the stake, found the thong that bound the white bird's leg, whispered, "Handbright? Handbright? It is Mavin, your sister."

There was no whispered answer, only the glare of mindless bird eyes, gleaming a little in the light of the embers. Well and well. It was a thing known to Shifters. Sometimes one took a form too long, too well, and could not leave it again. Well and well, sister, she thought. So you are sister no longer. Still, because of what you were and your protection of me. . . .

The serpent's form bound about the white bird, grew little teeth to chew the thong away, slithered away into the night to lead the white bird stumbling in the dark to the forest's edge as though it had forgotten how to Shift eyes for night vision, only the maddened gleam showing. "Stay," Mavin murmured, as she would have to some half wild fustigar. "Stay. I will return."

Then she returned to the stake, began to take on bulk, eating the grass, the leaves of the trees, whatever offered. At last, when she was ready, she trembled the stake and let the nets fall over her howling.

The hunter tumbled out of sleep, half dream-caught yet, snatched up a torch and thrust it into the embers, then held it high, uncertain whether he still dreamed or was awake, to confront the devil eyes within his gauzy net, to see the claws which shredded that net, the fangs which opened in his direction. . . .

Mavin thought, later, that perhaps he stopped running when he reached Mip, though he might have gone all the way to Hawsport. It had been a good joke.

Too good. The white bird had been no less terrified and had flown. All the search had to begin again, be done again. Still, when next she heard word of the white bird, that word had been clear. The white bird had flown west, over the sea.

Over the sea. To strange lands and far. To this chasm. Outside the wind had dropped. Through the woven gate she could see the glowing lanterns emerging from the root wall. It would not be long before the whatevers sought to fill their strange, manshaped garments once more. She sat up, seeing Mercald's eyes in the fishlight.

"You didn't wake me, Priest?"

"I was wakeful enough for us both, Mavin. I knew you would be about as soon as the wind dropped. I will sleep in a while, perhaps, while the Thinker keeps watch. If you need me—though I do not suppose you will—call me."

"Ah," she thought. "So you are still unhappy with me, Mercald."

She sidled out through the gate, surrounded at once by a great cloud of blue fish. Across the clearing, one of the flattree garments moved purposefully toward her.

Chapter 9

"You are not Mirtylon," she cried.

The balloon dress, twitchy upon its framework, stopped where it was, trembling in indecision.

"You are not Mirtylon," Mavin cried again, "but that doesn't matter. You do not have to be Mirtylon to talk with us."

"Am Mirtylon," it puffed *Ahhm Muhhrtuhh-lohhn*.

"No." She moved across the clearing, thrusting her way through a cloud of importunate fishes to stand beside it, almost within touch. "No. You ate Mirtylon. Now that you have eaten Mirtylon, you think Mirtylon. You have his name and can use it if you like. But you are not Mirtylon. What did you name yourself *before* Mirtylon?"

There was only an edgy silence during which the balloon quaked, shifted, and did not answer. At last an answer came, from another of the forms.

"No name . . . had no name . . ."

"Ah. Well. If you did not call yourself by human

names, what other name would you have?" The
Thinker had suggested this line of questioning in an effort to determine whether the things thought at all,
whether they could deal with conditional concepts.
Everything the creatures had said until now might have
been mere stringing together of phrases the humans
might have said—or so the Thinker thought. She
waited. Silence stretched thin. She could feel the
Thinker's eyes, behind her in the cave, watching every
tremor.

"We . . . bug . . . sticky."

Mavin's mouth fell open. What in the name of the
Boundless or any other deity was she to make from
that? She heard the Thinker hissing from the cave. "See
if you can get it to come out of that cover! Let us get a
look at it."

"Come out of that shape," she commanded.

"No." The word was strong, unequivocal, from
several of them at once. "No. Ugly."

She scratched her head. "Ugly" was a human word
and therefore represented a human opinion. Which
meant it was possibly what the dwellers of Waterlight
had thought of these creatures. Which had a great many
implications. "Ugly is all right," she said at last.
"Thinker is ugly." She waved at the cave behind her.
"Many things are ugly."

"Ugly . . . things . . . are . . . bad." *Ahhhr bahhhd*.

"Not . . . always." She shook her head, understanding what horror these words conveyed. She could
visualize what had happened on Waterlight bridge. It
would have been night, people would have been asleep,
then would have come the invasion of these whatevers,
the terror of being eaten alive, consumed, only to find
after one had been eaten that thought and personality
did not end but went on, and on, and on. Still, there
must have been some self-awareness in the creatures
before. Otherwise they could not have named themselves at all.

"All things which eat us are ugly-bad. Being eaten is
ugly-bad. If you do not eat me, I do not think you are

ugly-bad.'' There, let them chew on that, she thought, turning to rejoin the Thinker. "What do you think?"

He shrugged. "I postulate mentation prior to their having eaten people. However, seemingly they had no visual or aural symbolic communication. They obviously had some form of language, however, and it may have been in smell. They had a concept of number—the thing said 'we.' They had a concept of otherness—it said bug. They had a concept of relationship—sticky. It's possible we'll find they're a kind of mobile flypaper.

"However, if the people of Waterlight used the phrase 'sticky-bug' then these creatures may just be using it because they swallowed it. In that case, all we're left with is the fact one of them used a plural."

"All of which means?" sighed Mavin, understanding about one word in five.

"That I can't say at this point how intelligent they are, leaving aside for the moment that we don't know what intelligence is. I have always eschewed the biological sciences for exactly that reason; they're unacceptably imprecise." He peered over her shoulder, eyes suddenly widening.

Mavin turned. Something was flowing out at the bottom of the balloon dress, something thick and oleaginous, shiny on the top, puckered here and there as though the substance of it flowed around rigid inclusions. When it stopped flowing, it was an armspan across, ankle high, and it quivered. Out of the center of it, slowly edging upward as though by terrible effort, came the shape of an ear, a bellows. The ear quivered. The bellows chuffed. "Not . . . eating . . . you . . ." it puffed. "Not . . . ugly . . ."

While Mavin considered that, trying to think of something constructive to say next, a cloud of small flutterers swept through the clearing. As though by reflex action, the thing that had spoken lifted a flap of itself into their path. Wings drummed and struggled. There was a momentary agitation of small bodies upon the surface of the thing, then the smooth shininess of it closed over the disturbance.

"What did I say?" asked the Thinker, triumphantly. "Mobile flypaper!"

"Not ugly," said Mavin, firmly, trying not to laugh. "Very neat, very good-looking. Very shiny. You are . . . Number One Sticky."

Across the clearing another puddle of glue thrust up its own ear and bellows. "I . . . Number . . . Two . . . Sticky."

"Well, that answers a lot of questions," said the Thinker. "They certainly have self-awareness."

"And they can count," commented Mercald. "So, it is not beyond the bounds of possibility that they . . ."

"I don't want to hear it," said Mavin. "There isn't time. Whether they are religious or not, Mercald, I don't want to consider the matter now."

"Well. So long as you don't expect them to do anything that would offend against . . ."

"I don't want to hear that, either, Mercald. My understanding of what would offend against the Boundless is at least as good as yours. As you would remember if you reflect upon recent history!" Mercald flushed and fell silent, obviously distressed. Mavin turned to see the ears quivering at full extension, and cursed herself for having yelled. Undoubtedly she had confused them. "Pay no attention to the arguments we humans have from time to time. It is our way. Often, it means nothing."

"We . . . remember," the blob said. "Number . . . Two . . . Sticky . . .?" it repeated with an unmistakably questioning rise in tone.

"Number Two Sticky," agreed Mavin. "But you will have to mark yourself somehow, so that we will know which one you are. We cannot smell the difference as you probably do. We must see it."

Ears and bellows disappeared into the flat surface. The blobs quivered, flowed toward one another, seemed to confer through a process of multiple extrusions and withdrawals. Finally the surfaces of both began to roll from the bottom upward, breaking off to form a dull, fibrous pattern against the overall shine. The figures were clear, a large figure "1," an even larger figure "2."

"They've moved some of their bottom membrane onto their tops," said the Thinker. "That stands to reason. They couldn't move around at all if they were sticky on the bottom."

The conference among the Stickies went on, and more numbers began to appear, 3, then 4 and 5 in quick succession. When all those in the clearing had identified themselves, there were fifteen.

"Handsome," announced Mavin in an approving tone. "Very handsome. Very useful."

"And very fortunate that the poor people of Waterlight were literate," sighed Mercald. "I wonder if any of these creatures ate the babies on Lostbridge. Poor things. They wouldn't have enough language yet to talk with us."

"There . . . are . . . more. . . ." said One, breathlessly. "In . . . the . . . place we . . . stay."

"How many?" asked the Thinker. "How many of you?"

The glue blob quivered, shivered, erupted in many small bubbles which puckered and burst, then became calm, slick, only the fibrous identifying number contrasting upon its surface. The bellows gasped, puffed hugely: "Three thousand . . . nine hundred . . . sixty-two now. One was . . . crushed in the last . . . wind."

"And that," said the triumphant Thinker, "proves they can reason with quite large numbers. Well. Most interesting."

"Do all talk human talk? All understand?" Mavin's keen sense of survival quivered to attention. How many people had there been on the lost bridge, after all? Surely not almost four thousand of them.

The ear drooped, the bellows pumped. "Only . . . four hundred . . . seven. All. We . . . want . . . ed . . . did want . . . did want . . . not now . . . understand . . . not now."

"What did you want?" asked Mavin, already sure of the answer.

"Did want . . . people . . . to eat. For . . . the . . . others."

"Noble," sighed Mercald. "Risking their lives to help their brethren. Giving it up when they learn it is a greater wrong. . . ."

"Mercald, I am not at all sure they have learned any such thing," Mavin hissed at him, cupping her hands around her lips and standing close so that the stickies should not hear her. "They have said they do not wish to be ugly. Very well. But they desire to acquire more of—well, whatever it is they acquired when they ate the people of Waterlight. They're outnumbered nine to one by those who speak only in smells. Now, no matter how ugly I might wish to avoid being, that kind of desire would speak strongly to me. We will do them a courtesy by not putting temptation in their way."

"Of course not," he said with offended dignity. "I wouldn't."

"Then don't adopt them, Mercald. Don't make them into some kind of Bottom-dwelling holinesses. I've had some experience with promises of expiation and reformation. I've seen what happens when people act on such promises prematurely. We must not risk our lives on some religious notion you may have." She realized she was glaring, panting, that her face was flushed. "Oh, foosh, Mercald. I feel like we've been arguing about this for days. Can't you simply leave the religious aspects of it alone until you can get back to Topbridge and have a convocation or something to decide what it all means." She turned away, sure he had not heard a word she had said.

She returned to the stickies. "We have come here to find the big beasts that are eating the roots." Mavin had started to say "Great, gray oozers," and had then remembered what Mirtylon, nee Sticky One, had called them. "Do you know about those big beasts?"

"Beasts . . . eat . . . stickies . . . too," puffed Sticky Seven, quivering in indignation.

"We put . . . rootsap . . . on them. . . ." puffed another. Mavin could not see its number, hidden as it was behind two or three others. "Make little . . . ones sick . . . die. . . .''

"There, you see!" demanded Mercald. "Our interests are similar. We can help them!"

"We're going to have to help one another," muttered Mavin. "Rootsap won't kill the big ones? Is that what you're saying?"

"Too big . . . " came the disconsolate reply.

"Can the net hold the beasts? Do the big beasts crawl around on top of the net?"

"Go on . . . top, yes." Puff, puff. "Sometimes, net . . . breaks . . . beasts fall . . . down ? . . . eat us. Crawl around . . . eat . . . everything." This was the same sticky that had spoken before. By extending her neck a little, Mavin could read its number. It was Sticky Eleven.

"How many beasts?" she asked. "Many?"

There was a quivering conference among the glue blobs, with much extrusion of parts and emitting of smells. At last number Eleven struggled to the front of the group. "Nine . . . big ones . . . left . . . near here. Sap . . . killed . . . little ones. Always had . . . little . . . ones here . . . making pretty stones. First time . . . big beasts . . . come here. They come from . . . down-chasm." Puff, puff, puff, collapse. Eleven thinned to a pancake, bellows pumping impotently.

Sticky One took up the story. "Eleven is . . . right. Nine big . . . ones . . . left."

All right, thought Mavin. I'll need to think about this. She turned to Mercald and the Thinker, hammering a fingertip into her palm. "Now's the time to negotiate. None of the three of us is a representative of the bridge people—I speak of the governance of them, Mercald, not their religion. So, we need to get Beedie down here promptly. As a Bridger, she should serve nicely as ambassador. I can think of a few things we can try, but the agreement needs to be between the stickies and the chasm people so that it can't be repudiated later by some collection of Banders or whatnots."

"I am glad to hear you say so," murmured Mercald.

"Whoever speaks for us should be open-hearted. There is too little love and trust in you for that. You are too cynical. I do not think you are a real messenger from the Boundless, Mavin. The white bird . . . your sister . . . now, she is a different matter. I can believe she is a messenger."

Mavin stepped back, stung, angry. *Ah, my sister,* she thought. *Poor, mad Handbright. Yes. She is a different matter indeed. Besides, she doesn't argue with you, you pompous, self-righteous idiot!*

Aloud, she said, "You have not heard me, Mercald. I'm sorry. I have tried to tell you there are dangers in the unknown."

"And opportunities," he said. "Opportunities to extend the hand of friendship, the hand of . . . "

"And I have asked you not to extend anything yet," she snapped. "Wait until Beedie and Roges get down here. I'll fetch them now and be back by the time it gets light. Just wait here, both of you, and don't . . . do . . . anything."

She cast one quick look in the Thinker's direction, remembering that he had not yet seen her change shape. Bidding the stickies loudly to wait until she came back, she drew upon the power of the place to Shift into the great bird-bat form she had put together which could fly even in the soggy air of the chasm. Around her the place grew chill. She saw the Thinker shudder with cold as he stared at her. As she lifted through the cold in a whoosh of wings, she heard him cry out behind her.

"Marvelous! Revolutionary! A verification of the ergotic hypothesis!"

"Oh, by Towering Tamor," Mavin muttered. "Now I've done it. He'll want to talk to me about how I do this, and I can't explain because when I try to explain or even think about it I can't do it at all!" Resolutely, she turned her mind to other things, not thinking about flying, as she circled upward toward the amber gleam of Beedie's fire.

As she came closer, however, she saw that it was the gleam of a torch they carried in a headlong dash down the stairs. She Shifted into her own form and met them.

"Mavin!" cried Beedie. "Whoosh, I'm glad it's you. There's a hundred Banders clumping down behind us, and I wanted to warn you. I know you told us to stay put, but we didn't expect so many."

"A hundred?" Mavin was doubtful. "Surely not so many as that."

"One hundred seven," said Roges, putting down his pack in order to stretch his arms. "When we heard them coming, Beedie went back up to a place she could count them as they crossed a break in the stair. One hundred seven of them, each with much cursing and many weapons. They think they are to find some great treasure down below, something the Beeds and Chafers have kept secret from them for generations."

"You're right," admitted Mavin. "I expected neither so many nor so soon. Let me carry part of that for you. I think we'd best hurry to get as far ahead of them as possible. Throw the torch over; it will go out on the net below. The fish make enough light. Come. . . ." She led them on down, carrying some of their burdens so that all could move faster, ignoring all attempts at conversation.

When they had come some little way, she left them in order to fly up along the stair and see the descending Banders for herself. There were over a hundred, as Roges had said, old Slysaw in the forefront, all galumphing down at a steady pace and cursing the stairs as they came. She hovered just out of their sight, listening to their mutinous threats as to what they would do if they were not allowed to rest soon, then dropped on her bat wings down the chasm once more with a feeling of some relief.

"You've gained good distance on them," she told the others. "And they'll soon stop to rest. Evidently they've been climbing in the wind, and even though many of them have strong Bridgers' legs, they are tired and hungry. Come, give me that pack again, and we'll go a bit more slowly."

Beedie refused to relinquish the pack until she was

told what Mavin and the others had found in the depths. Then there were squeals of astonishment at the description of the stickies and still greater astonishment when she was told they would soon meet Mirtylon and Love-wings—or what remained of them.

"The Thinker is ecstatic at all the new theories he has about them," said Mavin. "But Mercald is determined that they are something very holy, somehow sanctified through guilt or some such. I have begged him to simply wait until we know a bit more before doing anything, but he accuses me of cynicism."

"Mercald is such an uneven person," said Beedie. "He can be brave as a pombi if it is a question of faith in the Boundless, and in the next minute he is peeing in his pants because he has the down-dizzies. I hope he will listen to you, Mavin, because I think he is not very realistic."

"And I hope you've had time to discuss a few things besides theology," panted Roges. "We may have gained on the Banders, but they will arrive at the Bottom eventually. When they do, they'll expect to do away with us, I imagine."

"I have a few ideas," said Mavin modestly. "A few things that might work out." Her foot jolted upon the solid floor of the chasm, and she sighed with relief. "Follow me. I've found a shorter way than the one we were led in by."

She led them at a fast trot through the whiskery halls beneath the net, pointing out the features of the place as she did so; the boiling pools—including one very large, deep pond alive with steam—the flopperskin kites that dotted the net, the ankle-high holes connecting between the hallways. Though her way was much more direct than the path the stickies had led them before, daylight was shining through the flattrees on the rim when she brought them into the clearing to find—no one. No Thinker. No Mercald. No stickies.

"Now what?" Mavin sighed in frustration. "Where have they gone? I told them to stay right here. I begged them not to do anything until I returned."

Roges moved through the open gate into the cave. "Here's the Thinker behind the door," he called. "He seems to be Thinking."

The others came in to see him crouched against the wall behind the gate, gesturing to himself as he babbled a string of incomprehensible words over and over. "Thinker!" Mavin demanded. "Where's Mercald? What happened to Mercald?"

"Mercald? Does one care? When one has verified the ergotic hypothesis at last, does one care about Mercalds? It seems that in order to describe the statistical state of a system, one needs an ensemble. There are those who believe the ensemble has physical reality, that the occurrence of a particular state corresponds to the frequency with which one observes the phenomenon. Others think the ensemble only a mathematical construct. It is now established that all systems must go through all states in the ensemble. Ergo, you can fly. This place is merely a rare event, sitting out in the tail of distribution of all places, non-representative. . . . I shall present a paper before the physical society at the fall meeting. . . ."

"Oh, flopper poop," said Beedie. "He saw you change shape, didn't he? He doesn't believe in the Boundless, like Mercald; and he isn't open-minded, like Roges and me; so he's theo . . . theor . . . thinking his way through it and has dropped off his bridge completely. He probably thinks I'm a rare event too, and no more real than anything else." She shook him. "Thinker! Where's Mercald? Tell me about Mercald!"

"Absolution," grated the Thinker distractedly, his eyes unfocused. "He wanted to give absolution to Sticky One. He wanted to lay on his hands in forgiveness, and he did, and he couldn't take his hands off, and he . . . ah . . . wah . . . aaahhh dissolved . . . aaahhh slurp!" The last word was uttered with a hideously descriptive sound which made them all recoil in disbelief.

"By the Pain of Dealpas," moaned Mavin. "By the Great Flood and the Hundred Devils. By the p'natti of my childhood. By . . . by . . . " She stuttered her way into silence, beating her head with one hand.

"A paper for Physical Review would be out of the question," muttered the Thinker. "It would never get by the idiot referees."

"By the Boundless," Mavin sighed at last. "Did Mercald think they had voluntary control over their stickiness?"

"I don't imagine he thought at all," murmured Beedie sadly. "Often he didn't, you know."

"Don't speak of it as though it were in the past," Mavin urged. "If he has been slurped up by Sticky One, he is still with us, still Mercald, and he will have a lot of time to consider what he has done." *Oh, Mercald, I told you to be careful. Because I did not speak in syrupy words, you would not listen.* She shook her head again, then laid down her pack and went out into the clearing.

"Sticky-One-Mirtylon-Mercald! Sticky Two! All the stickies! Come out, come out, wherever you are!"

Then she disgraced herself by weeping.

Beedie took her hand in sympathy. "It's awful, isn't it. I really want to throw up, but I haven't anything in my stomach at all."

Across the clearing the whiskery wall trembled. Moments passed. A sticky crawled out, slowly, so flat in aspect that Mavin wondered if it had suffered some accidental crushing. When it emerged completely, she saw that it was Sticky Two. "It's Lovewings," she sighed to Beedie.

"Sticky Two," she said, loudly, then waited for the ear to emerge, which it did only reluctantly. "I know what happened. It was not your fault. Not . . . your . . . fault."

"Sticky . . . One . . . fault . . . it was. . . ." puffed Sticky Two.

"No. It wasn't any sticky's fault," Mavin sighed. "It was the man's fault. He didn't think. Where is Sticky One, now?"

"Very . . . sick. Sticky . . . One has . . ." There was a long, long pause. "Has . . . too many . . . things inside

. . . all at once.'' The ear trembled, retracted, the bellows sighed dismally to itself.

"I'll bet he does,'' said Beedie. "Can you imagine trying to digest Mercald? Oh my, I shouldn't joke about it. But then, it shouldn't seem funny, and it does.''

"Sticky Two.'' Mavin was trying not to hear what Beedie said, for it made her want to laugh unbecomingly. "There are ugly men coming. We must do things very quickly. We cannot wait for Sticky One, or anything else. We must talk with all the speaking stickies at once. Please. Will you fetch them?''

The glue blob dithered for a moment, then flowed away under the wall. Roges came out of the cave nibbling on a piece of bread, offering some to Mavin and Beedie with the other hand. "Thinker is all tied up in knots talking to himself about you, Mavin, and birds and some law or other he claims you broke. I haven't seen him like this before, and I don't think he'll be much use to us.''

"That's all right,'' Mavin replied distractedly. "At least he'll be out of the way.'' She began explaining to Beedie and Roges what she had thought they might do, with much waving of arms and pointing here and there. Roges did not accept it without question.

"That's dangerous for Beedie, doer-good. She could be hurt!''

"She won't be, Roges. I'll take care of that part myself.''

Beedie had a doubtful comment. "You know how Mercald would feel about doing it this way. We still don't have any proof he would accept that the Banders are what we know they are.''

"He's not in any position to complain about it,'' she laughed bitterly. "We can give the Banders fair warning, if that would make you feel better. They won't heed it, but we can try. Then, if it's the wrong thing to do, Mercald can figure out later how we can expiate for it. All of us, including the stickies who help us do it.''

"Are you sure they will help us?''

"Well, sausage girl, it's up to your eloquence. I think

there's a good chance for building excellent relations with the stickies. If they do the chasm people a favor, then they'll be in good odor with all. If we do the stickies a favor, they'll want to treat us well in future. It's up to you, Beedie. You've been reared to work on the roots, to manage a crew. Now we need you to work on the root net, and the stickies will be your crew. Right now I think they're very eager to please. Let's see how eloquent you can be!"

At almost midday the Banders came down to the vast net which spread across the chasm, making a ceiling above the Bottom. The net was made up of many ropey roots, tugged sideways from the forest of verticals, which were knotted or grown together at armspan intervals, again and again, until the whole chasm was divided horizontally by a gridwork of thick, strong lines. Each individual polygon of rope-sized roots was further connected by a finer mesh of knotted root hairs. When Beedie had first seen it, she had known at once it was sufficiently strong to catch something large and flat dropping from above or perhaps even a person who might fall on his face while running across the grid. She had known at once it would not stop large rocks plunging from the rim—or the crawling gray oozers whose weight had torn ragged holes in the fabric already.

It was not unlike the floor of a bridge before the main planks were laid, and the Banders looked across it as a natural and familiar arena for exploration, whereas the Bottom, with its steams and stinks, was both strange and intimidating. Only one small group of the Banders went to the Bottom, found themselves in the maze of hallways, and promptly rejoined the others above the net level where they stood peering at the distant root wall, wondering where to go next.

It was not long before one of them, more sharp-eyed—or more acquisitive—than the rest, spotted a bright sparkle on the net, bounced his way out to it, and brought it back to be passed around among the others.

"Jewels," shouted Byle. "Dah, it's jewels. Laying

there on the net like so much flopper flub. See yonder, there's another sparkle.''

The gems, in glittering clusters, had been glued onto the grid with rootsap to form a twisting path. They were stones like those Mavin had discovered in the cave—gizzard stones from the small oozers, polished to a fine, high shine by the tumbling of the creatures' great guts. All the stickies who spoke human language had been at the labor of placing them until moments before the Banders arrived. Now the stickies crouched upon the net, and their shiny tops camouflaged with nonsticky bottom membrane, half-hidden with bits of root hair and leaf. The trail of gems wound out across the chasm; some of the younger Banders were already following it and collecting them.

Slysaw bellowed at them. "You all get off there! I didn't say go, and you don't go till I say. Now get back here and let me look at those. Well, well, what a wonder. So this is what the Birder and the Beedie wench were after. I'll be dropped off a bridge by my ears if this isn't something. . . ."

There were mutterings from the others in the band. One or two looked as though they were going to disregard orders, but these were cuffed into line by some of Slysaw's close kin.

"Now, boys. Now then. Think what a shortage of saw gravel there's been lately, and all the time pots of it here in the Bottom to be picked up by the pocketful! And won't we have fun taking all this back and showing it around. All this secret stuff the high and mighty Beeds and Chafers and Birders never told us about. Let's be orderly, now. Byle, you and your cousin get out there first, and the rest of us'll come after." And soon the hundred were moving across the net in a long line which undulated from side to side as jewels were found and picked and popped into pockets—though some were hidden in shoe tops or behind ears in the expectation of avoiding the eventual sharing out.

Up-chasm, others waited. Roges and Beedie were upon the net; Roges at the root wall, securely anchored

to a mainroot, Beedie more or less at the center of the
chasm, on the up-chasm side of the steamy place above
the boiling pool. Before her, and to either side, stickies
lay upon the net, almost invisible in the steam, their ears
carefully extruded between bits of leafy litter as they
listened for the signal.

Mavin, hovering high above, peered down through
the veils of steam. The mists made seeing difficult, but
she had planned for it to be difficult. She did not want
the Banders able to see clearly. They must be greedy,
angry, and with obscured vision. She lifted a bit higher
to see farther, then dropped down to whisper. "Beedie,
are you ready?"

Beedie waved her away impatiently, trying to remember her lines. At her direction, the largest, brightest
stones had been placed in the steamy place. Now she
could hear the result of that placement; raised voices,
argument, the sound of blows. She heard Slysaw's voice
as he intervened, his own greed making him half-
hearted. "Doesn't matter who finds 'em," he shouted
at his men. "We'll share alike when we're done. Just
keep gatherin' 'em in, and soon we'll come to the source
of it all. . . ."

The group tumbled on, stooping, grabbing, pushing
one another in their haste.

"Stop right there, Banders!" Beedie cried in a fine,
trumpety voice.

The men stumbled to a halt, their eyes widening in
surprise, searching through the steamy veils for the
source of the voice. Then one of them glimpsed her,
pointed, shouted. Behind him, others pushed close.

"Stop!" she cried again. "You have no business here,
Byle. Nor you, Slysaw. The rest of your ruffians should
be back at work on the bridgetowns that pay them. I
give you warning, you are at peril of your lives, so take
care. Go back to the stairs and up where you belong."

"And who're you, wench?" Slysaw thrust through
the pack, leaning on Byle's shoulder. "Who appointed
you head of chasm council, heh?" The Banders heaved
and pushed at one another, drawing into a smaller,

tighter group. Behind them stickies moved across the net.

"Yeah," interrupted Byle Bander, bouncing and posturing on the net. "Who're you, Beedie? I'll tell you. You're gametime for me, that's what. And after me, as many of these kin of mine as are interested in your skinny body."

Cheers and animal howls rose at this sally. Mavin, hearing this from above, recalled old, bad memories of Danderbat Keep, and boiled with fury. Still she hovered, close above the place Beedie stood.

"I tell you to go back. You are meddling in things that are none of your business. You do not belong here. You are in danger here. Don't be stupid, standing there threatening me. Just turn yourselves around and go!" Beedie no longer needed to remember lines she had rehearsed. She was now so angry that they came of themselves. Beside the root wall, Roges heard her anger and sizzled with protective wrath.

"We'll see, Beedie girl. We'll see. . . ." Byle plunged toward her through the rising steams, the entire pack pressed at his back. Slysaw was carried along in the rush even as his native suspicion made him try to stem the stampede. They came in a clot, all together, individually sure-footed yet stumbling against one another, so intent upon their own beastly mob noises they did not hear Mavin's scream.

"Stickies. Now. Now. Now. Now."

Roges at the root wall began to echo the sound, though Mavin's amplified voice could have been heard by any creature not deafened by its own howls. Beedie, too, cried out, and the three voices rose together.

"Now. Now. Now. Now."

Stickies had moved into a circle around the Banders, a circle that had already cut many of the main grid roots supporting the mesh above the boiling pool. Abruptly, with a loud, tearing sound, the fabric ripped to one side of the close-pressed mob. The flap of net they stood upon dropped to one side, throwing many of them flat, dropping others so quickly that arms and legs broke the finer meshes and dangled below, waving frantically at nothing.

Those at the rear of the pack nearest the torn edge were first to realize that there was nothing below but the sound of seething water, occasional glimpses of its bubbling surface appearing through the gusts of steam. Those who saw what lay below tried to climb over the bodies of those above them on the net, shouting and kicking. Those above them retaliated by kicking and pushing in return. Two or three men toppled through the hole and fell, screaming only for a moment before striking the water with a splash, a final agonized gargle and silence.

The entire pack was silent, only for that moment, not realizing what had happened but aware that something was wrong, that the net was no longer horizontal, that Beedie was moving away from them in the veiling mists, her face drawn into an expression of—what was it? Sorrow? Horror? At what? Even as shouts and howls arose once more, Byle, with his usual sensitivity, let voice follow wonder.

"Whatcha starin' at, bone body? Heh? Run if you like, Beedie, girl, but I'm faster than you are. . . ." Slysaw was grabbing at his shoulder, but the boy shrugged it off, blind and deaf to any needs but his immediate desire to do violence. Slysaw dropped and was trampled under the climbing hands and feet of a dozen others, kicked downward, beneath half a hundred struggling bodies, to lie at last half-dazed upon the very edge of the tear, clinging with both hands to a fine mesh of root hair.

The stickies had continued with their work. The tear widened, the finer lacework ripping with an audible shriek, ropey roots breaking under the increased weight with repeated, snapping sounds which made Beedie think of a drum rattling, faster and faster. "Go back," she screamed, unheard in the general din. "Go back." It was too late for any of them to go back, and she knew it only briefly before they did.

Now a second tear opened, across from the first.

Those who remained upon the net were caught now upon a kind of saddle, low at the sides, high at the ends, with those ends growing more narrow with each breath they took. Beedie stood just beyond one end so that she looked straight into Byle's face when the far, narrow strip broke through and the entire flap of net hung down for an instant's time, laden with clutching forms, shedding other forms amid shouted words she could not understand and some she could, old threats and obscenities, all ending in a liquid gulping, diminishing echoes, and quiet.

Beedie stood at the edge of the torn net, unable to move. Seeing her safe, Mavin dropped from her guardian's post through the roiling steams, past fringy edges of torn net and the quivering stickies poised there awaiting her word, down to examine the simmering surface of the pool. Nothing floated in it. She had not measured its depth, but now knew it must be a vast cauldron to have swallowed so many without a sign remaining.

Above, where Beedie stood, the net bounced from some weight hanging below it which jiggled and fought against falling. She looked between her feet to see him hanging upon a remaining shred of root just as his hand took her by the ankle. Byle Bander. She screamed his name.

And Roges drew his knife, cut the root hairs which fastened him safe at the root wall and ran upon the gridwork, sure-footed as any Bridger, not looking down, not remembering to be afraid, thinking of nothing except the sound of her voice. He came to her while she still struggled against the hands that were pulling Byle Bander upward on her body while he cursed at her and called her filthy names.

Beedie's cry had summoned Mavin back in that instant. She was too late. Her great bird's beak was too late to strike those climbing hands away. Roges' knife had already done so, and he stood with Beedie wrapped in his arms on a net which shook and shivered and threatened to collapse beneath them at any moment.

"Come on, young ones," she said quietly. "There's

other time for that, and better places." And she led them back to the root wall and down, not letting either of them go until she was sure they were safe.

Later, when they thought of it, they went looking for the Thinker. They could not find him. Mavin was suspicious of the stickies for a time, but they convinced her of their innocence at last. He had gone, gone as he had come, into some other place, through some wall only he could see or understand.

"Now I'll never know how I do it," Mavin thought with some disappointment. "I really thought he'd figure it out and would explain it to me." The disappointment was not sufficient to keep her from curling up upon the cave floor and sleeping for a very long time.

Chapter 10

It was some days later that they sat in the small commons room of Bridgers House on Topbridge. Beedie and Roges were unpacking a small bag they had brought from the Bottomlands, laying the contents upon the table before Rootweaver's interested eyes. Old Quickaxe sat in one corner where his blanket-wrapped body could catch the last of the day's light through a grilled window. Mavin sprawled before the hearth, playing with a stick in the deadroot fire which burned there to warm their supper.

"And you think all the great oozers are dead?" asked Rootweaver, fingering the gems on the table. "Though you did not see them killed?"

"We saw the first two killed," said Mavin. "The first time wasn't very efficient. The stickies hadn't quite figured out what smells were most attractive to the beasts, so the first one tended to wander about. The second time—"

"The second time was perfect," said Beedie. "They stretched a net-road right over the Stew Pot, that's what we named the boiling pool. Then they laid stink all over it, to attract the oozer. Then more stink to where the nearest oozer was, and it wasn't close at all. It must have come a long way. Then, when it went out on the net-road, they cut the net, and down it went. Stewed beast. That didn't smell very good either, but eventually it will all wash away."

"The stickies will have killed them all by now, ma'am," said Roges, "even the one we saw on the root wall above Bottommost. The Bridgers from Bottommost were driving it down into the chasm with torches when we came that way. Evidently there was only the one who climbed that high, and both they and the stickies were very eager to have the beast gone."

"Why now?" quavered Quickaxe from his corner. "What brought the huge beasts into the chasm? We have never had anything eating the roots before."

Mavin nodded in time with the dance of the flames. "I knew you would want to know, so I went down the chasm to see. There had been a rock fall there, just beyond the bend of the chasm. Evidently, a few of these very large beasts were trapped on this side of the fall. There are many of them farther down, where it is even wetter and warmer and where a different kind of vegetation flourishes."

"But you say there are small ones below us?"

"Not the same kind," said Mavin offhandedly. "The little ones are a different beast entirely. They don't eat the roots deeply, for one thing, and they stay away from the stickies, for another. The stickies have been killing them off with rootsap as long as any one of them can remember—certainly long before they ate the people on Waterlight."

"And it was gizzard stones they traded with the Waterlight people long ago?" Quickaxe asked.

"Gizzard stones, from which our saw gravel is made, yes. And our supply of it had been laid up since that time. Even hoarded and used thriftily, as we did, it would soon have been completely used up. . . ." Rootweaver sighed. "Now there is enough of it we may deck ourselves in gems as in the old stories."

"They traded different kinds of fungus, too," offered Roges. ''And fish lanterns. Things like that.''

"We made a treaty with them,'' said Beedie. "I hope the chasm council will ratify—is that the word, Mavin?—ratify it. The stickies won't hurt us if we don't build a bridge below the level of Bottommost, because it isn't wet enough for them that high up in the chasm. And if we aren't silly, like poor Mercald, and try to touch them, they can't do us any harm.''

Mavin nodded in agreement. "I think you can act on that assumption, ma'am. But take my warning. There are thousands of them down there that still speak in stinks, and they would really like to have living, thinking humans to eat. I don't think they're evil, but I don't think they're holy, either, and I'd continue to be careful.''

"Poor Mercald,'' sighed the old man. "I remember his father. No practical sense at all. Still, Mavin, there is a certain temptation there.''

Mavin rose slowly, looked the old man in the eye, thought carefully before she spoke. "Old sir, I will not presume to guide you. But before I would consider any such thing, I should have myself carried to the Bottom, and there I would speak with that which was Mercald. He is a confusion now, some Mercald, some Mirtylon, and some Sticky One. Still, he has gained . . . insight.''

Beedie and Roges both looked horrified when they finally realized that the old man meant that he felt a temptation to do what Mercald had done, but Rootweaver considered the idea calmly.

"Did he say anything to you? Mercald, I mean. Before you left?''

"He said he could find very little guilt or expiation in Mirtylon. And he said Mavin had been right. And he sounded very disappointed,'' said Beedie. "I felt so sorry for him I forgot and almost patted him on his shoulder.''

"He also said,'' Mavin spoke for the old man's ears alone, almost in a whisper, "that it didn't hurt. It surprised him, of course, since he wasn't expecting it. But it didn't hurt.''

The old man gave Mavin a fragile, tremulous smile. "If one were to do such a thing, one would have to do it fairly soon. While there is still time."

Mavin did not answer. She had found a great poignancy in Mercald's disappointment. His voice had puffed out of the sticky shape as all sticky voices did, windy and full of huffs, but the intonation had been very much his own. She recalled he had told her she had too little kindness in her, and this made her sad. Perhaps he was right. She had power, and had used it, and had made her own judgments. She did not regret them. But still . . .

She remembered the weeping children of Landizot.

The frightened hunter of Mip.

The slim, silver-horned beast she had loved in the pool-laced forest.

"What are you thinking about, Mavin?" Beedie whispered to her.

"I am thinking, sausage girl, that I wish Handbright would hurry with what she is about so that I may take the baby and go. Being among you has made me doubt myself, and that makes me fractious."

"Oh, pooh. You mean Mercald. That was his job, Mavin. Birders are supposed to make us doubt ourselves so we don't get too proud. Do you think you are too proud?"

Mavin shook her head, seeing Rootweaver's eyes on them from across the table. "Perhaps I was."

The older woman nodded. "Sometimes each of us is. Now, I think from the smell that food is cooked. Will you share it around, Roges?" And she rose to seat them all at the table.

They were only half through the meal when a Maintainer woman entered, beckoning Rootweaver into the hall. She returned with a sad face. "Your sister is not young, Mavin. Among our people, we would not want to bear children at her age."

"She's almost forty," said Mavin. "Is there trouble?"

"The birther women are concerned, worried. She has

been in labor for a very a long time now. She does not seem concerned. She sings, and does not concentrate. She seems to feel nothing. We have medicines, but they are dangerous. . . ."

"Well," Mavin rose. "I will come. No—alone. Beedie, you stay here. I'll see if I can help her, but I must do it with as few people around as possible."

Handbright was lying on a white bed, her legs drawn up, the muscles in her belly writhing, but her face was as calm as a corpse as she sang a little, wordless song. Mavin motioned the women out of the room, asking only the head birther to stay. The place smelled of the sea, salt and wet.

"Tell me what she must do," she directed the birther, taking Handbright's head between her hands to make the blind eyes stare into her own. She began to speak. It was the voice she had used in Landizot and in Mip; the voice she had used on the Bander mobs, utterly confident and compelling.

"Handbright. White bird. Shifter. Sister. You have seen birthing before. This is a good child. Like Mertyn, Handbright. Mertyn. Mertyn. A good child. You must save this good child, you must birth it, Handbright. Think." The birther woman gestured, thrusting down. "Push. Birth the good child."

Something fled behind Handbright's eyes, the singing stopped. Mavin went on, demandingly. "Save this good child, Handbright. Concentrate. Push. Think. This is a good baby. Handbright always wanted a baby. Think. The birther says now, Handbright. Push. See. That makes it easier. Now again, push."

Handbright cried out, a sound completely human rather than the strange birdsongs she had made before. The birther nodded, encouraged, and felt the swollen belly. Mavin spoke on, and on, and on.

There was a thin cry, and she looked down to see a wriggling form, all blood and wetness, in the birther's hands. Sighing, exhausted, she released her sister's hands and sat back. There was a scurrying. Others came in from the hallway. Handbright cried out once more and the birthers moved even faster around the bed, lifting another child in their hands. Mavin looked on only, bewildered.

"Twins," cried one. "Twin boys."

"Ah, now, now," thought Mavin, tears in her eyes. "One would have been quite enough. More than enough." She rose unsteadily and went out into the hall, breathing deeply. She had seen death in Handbright's eyes. If not now, soon. Soon. Well, she could have come more quickly. She could have interfered less in the world's business and paid more attention to her own. She leaned against the wall, weeping, not knowing Beedie was there until she felt the strong young arms tight around her.

The birther came into the hall, her face strained and tight.

"Never mind," said Mavin. "I know."

"She's asking for you," the birther said. "She's come to herself. She's asked for the babies, too."

"Well then," Mavin responded. "Well then."

She sat in that quiet room for the rest of the day, and most of the day following. The birthers put Handbright's children to her breasts, though she had no milk for them yet and none of them expected that she would have. Still, she asked to have them. And Mavin. She talked of Mertyn and their mother. And died, lying quietly there with the babies in her arms.

The Birders came the next day, expecting to send Handbright's body to the Boundless. Mavin told them it had already gone.

"What are their names?" asked Beedie, poking one of the babies with her strong, Bridger fingers to make it smile.

"Swolwys and Dolwys," said Mavin. "Dolwys has hair that is a little darker, I think."

"Will you let me have them?" asked Beedie, all in a rush. "Me and Roges. We decided together we'd like to have them. We'll have some of our own, too, of course, but we'd like very much to raise Handbright's sons."

"No, sausage girl. You'll have enough of your own to keep you busy. These are my own kin, my own Shifty kin, and they will need to be reared by those who understand our ways. I'll take them with me, as soon as they are a tiny bit older and able to travel."

"How will you carry them, Mavin? How can you manage with two?"

"I'll manage," she said. "I'll figure out a way."

It was in the summer season that the people of Battle-fox the Bright Day, a Shifter demesne on the high downs of the shadowmarches, looked out across the p'natti to see a great beast. The beast would not have been considered extraordinary by any Shifters' demesne. Shape and size and aspect are all infinitely variable in Shifters' lives, and they are not surprised by fur or fang or feather. Still, there was something surprising about this beast: the red-haired twin boys who rode upon its back.

The beast opened its mouth and bellowed, "Plandybast!" at which one of the inhabitants of Battlefox Demesne trembled with mixed apprehension and delight.

By the time he had threaded his way through the p'natti, Mavin stood there in her own shape, holding the toddlers by their hands. "Plandybast," she said. "Thalan. My mother's brother. You told me once Handbright would have been welcome at Battlefox Demesne. Tell me now that her sons are equally welcome!"

After which was a time of general rejoicing, story-telling, lying, and welcoming home. Plandybast's half sister, Itter, had left the Demesne long before and was believed to be dead. Mavin sighed with relief and offered polite consolation. Itter had been the one thing she had doubted about Battlefox Demesne. Now there was nothing to doubt, and even Mavin herself felt at home.

Still, in a few seasons, after the babies were accustomed to the place and had found dozens of kin to care for them, she took quiet leave of the demesne.

"Can you tell me why you're leaving us?" begged Plandybast, who had grown fond of Mavin.

"Oh, thalan, you will think it a silly thing."

"I would rather be told and think it a silly thing than think myself not worthy of being told."

"Well then, hear a tale. Some almost twenty years ago, I came with Mertyn to Pfarb Durim. He was a child, and so was I, scared as two bunwits in a bush when the fustigars howl. So, we made it up between us I would say I was a servant of a Wizard. Himaggery. Mertyn made up the name."

Plandybast nodded. "Not a bad stratagem. Wise men don't fool with Wizards, or the servants of Wizards."

"That's what Mertyn thought. So, I told my tale, but during the next few days I came into danger and told my tale to unbelieving ears. Then came one who said, 'This is my servant, and I am the Wizard Himaggery.' "

"Ah," said Plandybast.

"And the end of the tale was I swore him an oath, thalan, that in twenty years time I would come once more to the city of Pfarb Durim, to find him there."

After a thoughtful silence, "Will you be back for Assembly?"

"Perhaps not then. But I will be back. I'll be back for the boys when they're old enough. I want to take them to Schlaizy Noithn myself, if they turn out to be Shifter. If they turn out to be something else—or nothing else—well, I want to decide what should be done in that event."

"Not the Forgetter?"

"No. Not the Forgetter. We have tried to convince the world we are . . . limited, thalan. So they would not fear us, or hate us. We have woven mystifications around us, and the world does not believe them. Shifters are not well liked in the wide world. That being so, why should we commit evil deeds to protect that which can't be protected?

"Ah, well. I don't intend to get the demesne in an uproar raising the question now. It'll be ten years or more before we know what Handbright's sons will be. It may be best to take them back oversea to their father's people."

"Who is their father?" asked Plandybast, curious about this matter for the first time.

Mavin thought briefly she would tell him, "A glue blob in the bottommost lands of a chasm, over the sea." Instead she contented herself with a larger truth. "A priest," she said. "A good and kindly if imperfect man."

She turned when she arrived at the bend in the road beyond which the demesne disappeared behind the hill. He was waving to her, smiling, weeping a little. Beedie had wept a little, too, and Roges, when she had left them. It was pleasant to be wept over in such kindly fashion.

And the better part of twenty years was gone since she had promised she would keep tryst in Pfarb Durim, twenty years from then.

And the better part of twenty years was gone.

"I am the servant of the Wizard Himaggery," she hummed, remembering that refrain. "Perhaps. Almost. But not quite yet."

BESTSELLING
Science Fiction
and
Fantasy

Stories
✤ of ✤
Swords and Sorcery

Prices may be slightly higher in Canada

Available wherever paperbacks are sold or use this coupon.
